An Innocent Soldier

by JOSEF HOLUB

Translated by Michael Hofmann

ARTHUR A. LEVINE BOOKS

AN IMPRINT OF SCHOLASTIC INC.

Fic
Holu

Library of Congress Cataloging-in-Publication Data

Holub, Josef, 1926–

[Russlander English]

An innocent soldier / by Josef Holub ; translated by Michael Hofmann. — 1st ed,

p.   cm.

Summary: A sixteen-year-old farmhand is tricked into fighting in the Napoleonic Wars by the farmer for whom he works, who secretly substitutes him for the farmer's own son.

ISBN 0-439-62771-0 — ISBN 0-439-62772-9 (alk. paper)

I. Napoleonic Wars, 1800–1815 — Campaigns — Russia — Juvenile fiction. [1. Napoleonic Wars, 1800–1815 — Campaigns — Russia — Fiction. 2. War — Fiction. 3. Russia — History — 1801–1917 — Fiction.] I. Hofmann, Michael, 1957 Aug. 25- II. Title.

PZ7.H74278Inn 2005   [Fic] — dc22   2005002583

10   9   8   7   6   5   4   3   2   1   05   06   07   08   09

Printed in the United States of America   23

First American edition, October 2005

Map illustration © 2005 by Kirk Caldwell

Historical Note

By the year 1811, Napoleon was ruler of a huge French Empire. His allies stretched across Europe, from Spain to Germany to Poland. But one of his allies, Czar Alexander of Russia, refused to adhere to Napoleon's strict system of controlling trade.

Napoleon decided to teach Russia a lesson. Starting late in 1811, he mustered his troops and called on the rest of his allies to supply as many soldiers as possible. About 450,000 men marched in the resulting force, called the *Grande Armée*. It was the biggest army the world had ever seen.

Despite being warned about Russia's severe winters and the enormous distances that had to be covered, Napoleon set out in the spring of 1812, confident that he would conquer the Russian Empire in a quick campaign. But the warnings proved to be correct. The food and supply wagons could not keep up with the huge army. Czar Alexander's generals confused the French military leaders with unconventional attacks. And the soldiers' thin uniforms and weakened conditions were no match for a viciously cold winter.

Less than a quarter of the hundreds of thousands of soldiers returned safely home.

I.

November 1811.

It's only barely after midnight.

The farmer has just shot me through the heart with his new hunting rifle. Only it doesn't seem to hurt. Perhaps the shot wasn't real, but just the mischief of a dream.

So I'm not really dead at all. Otherwise, I would hardly have woken to mull over these crazy night spooks. Just to get rid of the slightest doubt, I give myself a sharp pinch. I feel it, thank God. I am alive. Gratefully, I sit up on my straw mattress and blow the last of the dirty dream air from my lungs.

What causes a dream like that? If only I knew! No one thinks up these sort of things by himself, not in the daytime. What would possess the farmer to shoot me, his farmhand, through the heart? Stupidity? Desire to kill? Irritation? Not possible! Least of all, my farmer. He has to think a thing through at least twice before he does it

1

even once. Three years ago now, he took me on as his youngest farmhand. I'm not especially big and strong, but I work hard, and already I understand a thing or two about farming. There's really no reason to shoot me.

Stuff! It was just a dream. I turn onto my front and draw up my left knee against my belly.

But I can't relax completely. Leftover scraps of the old dream feed a new one. And once again, the farmer is involved. This time, he doesn't shoot me, he shakes and shakes me. He's so merciless about it that my bones rattle and my muscles twitch. I don't stir. What am I going to do against the farmer, anyway? Am I supposed to fight him off? Of course I'm not allowed to do that, not under any circumstances. Not even in my dreams. The farmer comes just after God and king. He gives me one or two more shakes, then he seizes me by the shoulders and pulls me bodily upright.

"Farmer," I groan. "What's the matter? What do I have to do?"

No more sleep. I rub my eyes awake. This dream is different from the last one. The farmer refuses to vanish, he stays there. He's hunkering down by my sack of straw, as large as life, and he's shaking me vigorously awake.

"Get up!" he commands me.

It's pitch-black, and the other farmhands are snoring away. Why am I the only one who has to get up?

"Has something happened?" I ask, half awake. "Is

Olga calving already?" But then I think, this can't be about Olga. She's not due for another four or five weeks. And even if she were calving now, it wouldn't be me but the oldest farmhand that the farmer would have come for.

"Splash some water on yourself, and put on your Sunday best," the farmer commands. "We're going into town."

"Into town?"

Did I hear correctly? Really — into town?

Into town. My heart starts to thump with happiness. What could be so important that the farmer drives into town with me?

Then it comes to me. Right! Could it be my birthday? It must be today or tomorrow, or perhaps it was yesterday or the day before. On one of those four days I must have turned or be turning sixteen. But that can't really be the reason.

"But who's to muck out the cow shed?" I ask back cautiously.

"Never you mind! I'll see to that."

He's right. The farmer's always right. He can get the cow shed mucked out by anyone he says and anytime he wants it done. Or if he decides he likes it better that way, he can leave it with the muck in it.

The farmer's wife is banging around in the kitchen. With a sour old face. She often looks like that. Especially

3

in the morning. Of course, she hasn't heard about my birthday, and so she doesn't offer me her congratulations. Not that she would congratulate me if she did know. There isn't much congratulating on this farm. No one in the whole village knows one jot about my birthday. Why would they? A person gets born, whether he wants to or not.

The pan with milk is already on the table. I wait obediently for the farmer to cut the bread. As usual.

"Cut your own," the farmer's wife says to me quietly.

The world is about to end, I think. Or is the violation of the bread rule something to do with my birthday, after all?

Something's amiss. Of course, I cut myself a big thick doorstop of a slice. I'm even allowed to put butter on it myself. Which I do equally lavishly. The farmer's wife makes big round eyes when she sees me, but she doesn't fuss, and she doesn't stop me.

"You eat!" she says. "Lord knows when you'll have something in your belly again."

"Will we be staying so long in town?" I venture to ask back. But no one gives me an answer. It's not fit for an apprentice to ask a cheeky question like that.

The farmer's wife never had to give anyone a second invitation to eat. She's more likely to put on the brakes. The farmhands always eat as much as possible. If there is

anything to eat. They had better be quick about it, too.
It's a matter of survival.

"Harness up the sleigh," orders the farmer.

"The sleigh?"

"You heard me, the sleigh!"

The horses are sleepy and lazy. They don't want to go
out in the cold, and I have to push them in front of the
sleigh.

2.

We set out, the farmer and I. Just the two of us.

The morning is dry and cold. Far too cold for November. Up in the mountains there's already lots of snow. What will it be like once the real winter comes? Behind the royal woods, a bit of light creeps into the eastern sky. In the valley below, there's now more day than night. Sleighs and carts have flattened out the snow on the road.

A wild joy creeps under my ribs and pokes out in places. In all my sixteen years, I have never once been to town. Of course, there was never any reason to. No one goes into town without a reason. Today, apparently, there is a reason. The farmer will know what he's about. Even so, I'd like to know, too. I wonder if it's so I can say my oath of allegiance to the king? But normally you don't swear oaths in town, but before the bailiff in Bohringsweiler. So it must be something else.

He is a good man after all, the farmer. Maybe he even likes me. It doesn't have to be a big, fatherly love. A little bit would be plenty. Toward a sort of second, alternate son. Because he's got one already, who is Georg. There might have been five by now. But there aren't. They all of them died except him. Either in infancy, or later on with scarlet fever, convulsions, or the quinsy. Apparently, the farmer's wife can't have any more children. "Her belly's completely wrecked!" That's what the stable boys and maids whisper to one another.

Now what if the farmer wants to have another son? Who's to say he doesn't? Then I'd be a candidate. Who knows? He's known me for three years already. For a little while now, I thought I could sense something like a little bit of affection coming from him. Even if the farmer's usually strict and brutal, and never uses two words where one will do. But then he doesn't talk much to his wife, or to Georg, his son, either. Anyway, it's me he's taking into town now. Who's to say that's not a good sign?

A new, incredibly big slice of the world lies ahead of me. Unfamiliar and exciting. I don't know where to look, so I look left and right and straight ahead, and paint the passing pictures in my memory. There's so much to look at. Tonight I'll tell the other farmhands all about it. I can see them all openmouthed with astonishment, but also with envy.

I wonder if the houses in town are really all stuck

together like stillborn calves? The farmhands and maids talk such nonsense sometimes.

It's late morning when we reach town. The snow on the roads gets thinner and mushier, and the sleigh scrapes against the stones quite often. That makes it difficult for the horses, and they're steaming with effort.

It's true that most of the houses are stuck together. Amazing. So they weren't kidding me after all. What all isn't possible? So many houses, and such a lot of people.

I wonder if I should tell the farmer how excited I am.

I peer at the farmer from the side. But he's just got his horse-faced expression on, and not a little bit of what he's thinking shows through. Probably better I don't say anything foolish to him. There's no knowing how he might respond to my blathering.

On both sides of the street, it's just one house after another, and none of them have decent dung heaps. That means the people who live in town can't be especially rich. Although the houses all look big and grand. Perhaps the rule about dung heaps in front of houses doesn't apply in town. Perhaps the people who live here are rich, even though they don't have any livestock.

All the time we were driving, the farmer didn't say a single word to me. Of course, that doesn't necessarily mean anything. He never talks much to the help. The hands and maids and laborers he just tells what to do, or else he shouts at them.

8

Then suddenly, he does speak to me. Two words. "Town hall!" he says, and he points at a high, gabled building that's taller than all the roofs around it. After a while he adds four more words, a bit more quietly: "That's where we're going."

To the town hall, I think to myself, but of course I don't ask the farmer why we have to go to the town hall. The farmer will know.

This town hall is a huge building. Fourteen windows on the front side alone. I wonder how many it has altogether — thirty or more?

There are heaps of soldiers standing outside the gate, and on the stairs, and on the second floor. Young men are coming and going the whole time.

The farmer and I hang around in a bay window for a while. Pointlessly, not doing anything. And that in the light of day. A pure waste of time! That's the way you rob the Almighty of His day. The farmer is restless. Something is bothering him. Can it be that he's afraid of the town hall or of all these people? Hardly. And with him being a village mayor and all. It would take more than a town hall to scare him.

And then, before long, the farmer's name is called. Not his, actually, but Georg, his son's. The farmer pulls a bundle of papers out of his vest pocket and goes into the room across the hall. Soon he comes out again, grabs me by the arm, and pushes me roughly through the door.

In front of me is an enormous table. Behind it are several soldiers all glittering in silver and gold. They're bound to be officers. They remind me of the captain of the militia who was billeted with us last year. They're all sitting there like roosters. Proud and disdainful. You can tell from looking at them that they must be important people in the kingdom.

What am I doing standing in front of these people? What do they want with me?

Fear seeps into me. I look nervously around for my farmer. But he's not there anymore. Gone! Why didn't he stay? Surely he wouldn't just leave me here on my own?

The farmer's bundle of papers is lying on the table.

"Georg Bayh," says one of the men, in a bored, nasal tone of voice. "Step forward!" Before I can reply, someone else hisses at me: "You gone deaf, boy?" And the man in the middle orders: "Strip!"

But I'm not Georg Bayh, I think to myself. I'm not him at all. Georg Bayh is the farmer's son. I'm only a farmhand, and my name is Adam Feuchter. Georg Bayh is at home. The farmer is going to come back any minute and explain the mistake.

I take another look around. The door is closed, and I don't see any farmer coming in. I want to go out in the passage and call him. But the gentlemen around the table are all looking at me incredibly severely and impatiently.

"Strip!"

Strip? What would I do that for? All these gentlemen want to look at me naked? I feel ashamed in front of so many men in fine uniforms.

The officer who has the papers lying in front of him roars: "Strip! We haven't got all blinking day!"

I look up at the men and then over to the door again. No farmer. Then I take off my clothes. I have no choice. It doesn't take long, either; after all, I've only got my tunic, shirt, and pants. And shoes. Thank God I washed quickly this morning.

So I'm standing there, bare naked, and the officers inspect me from top to toe, and back up again. As if they were buying bulls or horses.

One of them walks up to me. "Open your mouth!" he orders. He puts his hand in my mouth. His fingers smell of something nasty. "Teeth are fine," he says.

Another man says in a whining sort of voice: "There's not much of him." And another says: "Absolutely not. He's just a boy. Just look at him. It'll take a bit more to make a man of him yet."

"Turn around!"

I panic. Suddenly I know what this is. This is the conscription commission. They're the people from the military who travel around on the king's behalf, looking for soldiers for the army. I've often listened to the farmhands talking about how they came to be soldiers. They were inspected, just like this. And afterward, they had to serve in the army for eight or ten years.

With desperation, I yell out to the officers' table: "Stop! You've got the wrong person." Suddenly my mouth is full of spit. I gulp it down and choke, "I'm not —" It's as far as I get. Once again, my windpipe is blocked.

The men leap to their feet. One of them shouts so loud it makes his voice crack: "Who do you think you are, boy!" and another draws his saber and smacks me across the behind with the flat of it. "Speak when you're spoken to! And not otherwise! Got that?"

My behind feels as if it's on fire. I try to keep from crying, but I can't quite manage it.

The men behind the table look at one another angrily.

"It's high time that young pup was taught a lesson." Another one echoes him: "High time he joined the army! So he learns some obedience!"

But one of the officers doesn't agree with them.

"He's just a boy," he says in a quiet voice. "Just observe his skinny frame, his narrow chest. His voice hasn't broken, you can hear it squeaking and scratching. And other signs of adolescence . . . Well, see for your-selves. We don't want children in our army."

The other men exchange cross looks again, and the important officer, the one who has the farmer's papers in front of him, hisses furiously: "Gentlemen! Do I have to remind you that His Majesty requires troops? Urgently! In great numbers! This is no time to be fastidious."

The others all chorus: "Yes, sir! The king needs troops. This is no time to be fastidious." The important officer looks at one of the papers and gives a satisfied grunt: "All right then, gentlemen. Let's not jump to false conclusions! This fellow, what was his name again, Georg Bayh, has attained the prescribed age, and he's big enough too. That's what it says here, black on white."

"He may have attained the age, even if he looks more like an altar boy, but I assure you he's not big enough," objects the doubter once more.

"Then measure him!"

A soldier who's standing next to the table brings a measuring rod. "Five feet two inches, sir!" he reports.

"What?" yells the senior officer. The others all flinch.

"Not possible!" he barks, jumps out from behind the table, and stares at the measuring rod. "Ha, I've seen that before," he says bitingly. "Trying to make himself short, so that he doesn't get to wear the king's tunic. Head up now, chest out, knees straight!"

He pulls me up by the ears and then looks at the measuring rod again. "That's better," he says happily. "Well, there's not so much missing now. I want you to get up on tiptoe, got that?" It's stock-silent in the room.

Only my occasional sobbing bursts out. I can't help it. It comes up from the pit of my stomach. Everyone is staring at the measuring rod.

"Well, now! Five foot four. And the two little inches that are missing, he'll make them up soon enough, the little man. Gentlemen, see for yourselves. Anyone still require convincing? Or have you seen enough?"

The officers pull their heads in further between their shoulders. They are convinced. Just the odd uncertain glance passes between them.

"Fit for service," they pronounce, a little hesitantly, but all together.

"Now, get the little wretch out of here!" bellows the important officer. He takes the papers, smashes them on a pile of other papers on the edge of the table, and yells: "Next!"

I put my head down and make a mad dash for the door. The soldier with the measuring rod flings my clothes after me.

Bewildered and tearful, I stand in the corridor. Some people are laughing at me mockingly, but some are sympathetic. I must get out of here. Where's the farmer? He can clear this whole thing up in no time, and I'm sure he will. I jump into my pants and shoes, jam my shirt and tunic under my arm, and go bounding down the stairs.

"Farmer! Farmer!"

But the farmer isn't anywhere to be seen. Around the corner? Not there. Where has he got to? The sleigh and the horses aren't in the side alley. I stop in front of the town hall, not knowing where to go. I'm shivering. I still have my shirt and tunic wedged under my arms. My chest is covered with goose bumps. I must get away from town.

Up on the second floor, a window is pulled open. An officer shouts down to those below.

Four soldiers dash up to me.

"Halt!" they shout, as I make to turn down the next street. "Stop! Stay right there! You're coming with us."

"I want to go home."

"Nothing doing. Orders from the staff captain. You can't go home. You're a soldier now, and you're coming to the depot with us."

Sometime after noon I stop crying for the farmer. My sobbing is still with me, though. It gulps up from deep inside me.

3.

Early in the afternoon, about a dozen soldiers are marching me and a whole lot of other young boys in farm clothes out of town. There's powdery snow on the heights. Lower down in the valleys, it turns slushy. The slush is water and snow and plenty of mud, and it sloshes over the tops of our boots. The soldiers swear terribly. Each time the road goes through forest, they take the guns off their shoulders and level them at us.

I'm tired and hungry. I haven't had anything to eat since early this morning. At least it's not raining or snowing even.

It's getting dark as we head down into a river valley. "The Neckar," says one of the farm boys. He must know his way around here.

"Where are we going?" we ask him.

"What do I know? Ludwigsburg, I expect. There are a lot of barracks there."

One of the soldiers is more talkative.

"Right, you're all going to the reception depot in Ludwigsburg. There's going to be war again soon, and the king needs soldiers."

"Particularly for the French emperor, that Napoleon!" another adds softly and with awe in his voice.

Dismal thoughts weigh on my brain. What do I have to do with Napoleon? Why do I suddenly have to be a soldier now? Why didn't the farmer wait for me?

For an hour we climb through vineyards up to the heights. It's well dark by the time we pass through a big gate into a barracks yard.

I sleepwalk across the sandy expanse. There's no snow here, and not much slush, either. A lot of boot soles have dissolved it and left puddles of dirty water. An arrogant soldier with hat and saber marches up to us.

"Halt!" he yells. "Where are you going?"

"Recruits," reports one of our guards.

"Wait there."

A soldier mutters to himself: "When are we going to get some grub?" And the others take up the question.

We farm boys are all freezing. The soldiers are swinging their arms and smacking their shoulders against the cold. They're no better off than we are. I suppose their uniforms aren't much good in winter. Everyone's belly is grumbling. It's pointless standing in the empty yard like this. I need to go very badly, but I can't see how or where. I think of the farmhands' room and my straw sack. It would be reasonably warm in there now. And the dung heap would be outside in front of the cow shed. I could just nip down there and let loose. But there's no sign of any dung heap here.

Half the night must be over. It's begun to snow. A fat soldier comes waddling up to us. He yawns and looks at the group of us, trembling with cold.

"Come with me," he orders.

We walk right across the barracks yard toward a low building. Suddenly, I feel warmth. I revive out of my stupor. A stable. No doubt about it. Hoof scraping and lip smacking and the homey smell of straw and dung.

"No lighting a fire," the fat soldier tells us. "You can sleep in there for tonight. There's no more beds in the barracks."

"And when are we getting some grub?"

"Soon."

A little later, two soldiers come in carrying a bucket between them. It smells of broth and pickled cabbage and noodles, a good smell, a very good smell.

"What are we going to eat with? We haven't got any eating irons."

"There are some spoons there."

"What about plates?"

"What do you need plates for!"

Quickly everyone grabs a spoon, and we cluster around the bucket and start shoveling the stuff into us.

It's a thick mash of potatoes, beans, and other things, and it's not at all bad. With a bit of effort, I manage to get several spoonfuls into myself. There's a little scrap of bacon in one. I leave it in my mouth and enjoy the heavenly taste. But then I quickly gulp it down, because the other boys' spoons are already scratching the bottom of the bucket, and I have to hurry to get another dab or two of the mash.

Soon after, the spoon drops from my hand. I tip back into the warm straw. This time, the hole I fall into is so deep that I forget all about the wretched world around me. Even my thoughts about the farmer disappear as quickly as the three drops of honey in the acorn coffee we get on Sundays for a treat.

4.

In the reception depot, there are loads of soldiers and young boys on their way to becoming soldiers. Every day there are more. There haven't been any beds for ages now. Every little bit of room in the stables has been taken. Even outside the barracks, the recruits are sometimes put up in so-called double billets. That's two soldiers sharing a bed. While one sleeps, the other's on guard duty, and then turnabout.

Soldiers out of uniform get as little respect as bare-naked kings. So the new recruits are issued uniforms in double-quick time. They stick me in a uniform, too. It doesn't fit me anywhere, it smells of sheep droppings and tar soap, and it's not particularly warm, either. It's too thin for winter, but it's still better than my thin civilian Sunday tunic. It's pale blue from top to bottom, almost sky blue. The pants have room enough for two scrawny bottoms like mine. I get a longish pot stuck on my head, which they call a casquette, with a horsehair plume on top. That's the only part of my uniform that fits me at all. Thanks be to God, my boots only rubbed me sore in the beginning. I can manage to walk in them properly if I wrap the foot cloths around my toes and heels tightly enough so they don't slip.

Three weeks before Christmas, I bump into the son of Kleinknecht the laborer from the village. Kleinknecht is still in his civvies, and he's quite surprised to see me in the barracks.

"They're talking about you in the village," he tells me.

"What are they saying?"

"I don't know whether I should tell you. They say you stayed in town because you liked it there so much. Your farmer says he's not going to forgive you now, whatever you do."

"He won't? Why not?"

"Well, because you've stayed away too long."

And because he's in a great hurry, Kleinknecht runs off.

I'm all confused. The world has gone mad! I've stayed in town, and my farmer won't forgive me?

The barracks is like a typical town. There's a big open square ringed by stables and stalls and long two-story houses. On the edge there's a fancy house with sentries at the door and all sorts of gleaming officers going in and out. Those are the men who have a say, they all go by Your Honor or Your Grace, and there's even supposed to be a Your Excellency among them.

That's the house I have to get into, to tell the officers that I'm not really allowed to be a soldier at all because I'm only sixteen. If they don't believe me, then my farmer can settle it anytime. He's not just anyone, either, he's the mayor in the village.

But I don't dare go inside. Who am I going to tell about the mistake? No one would believe me. I need to think it through carefully. In the end, I don't get around to it at all. Sergeants and corporals and lieutenants and other soldiers dressed up with sabers are using up every minute of my life.

At first, I resist all the shouting and the senseless running back and forth. Picking up your feet, trudging around the barracks yard, standing around doing nothing — what sort of work is that? Just a lot of silly hocus-pocus. When they give especially stupid commands, I make a fuss and do the exact opposite. I quickly realize how foolish that is. The sabered ones don't take kindly to it. They tyrannize me till I don't know which way is up. I can't take it for very long. After a few days I'm forced into being an obedient soldier.

All I think is what the other soldiers think.

And soldiers don't think much. Certainly, they don't do any unnecessary thinking. They think of their straw sack when they're tired, and of food when their bellies are grumbling. All the life in between is pretty unthinking. Well, not entirely. When the soldiers have eaten, and if they're not being tyrannized, then they talk about buxom girls. Not that there are any of those in the barracks.

My muscles and bones remind me of their presence with tears and cramps and aches. My head gets emptier all the time. The switch from young apprentice to dutiful soldier comes on apace, almost inevitably. A person can get used to anything. I can, too.

The most important quality in a soldier is obedience. Irrespective of what he's told to do. And, after that, marching. You can do that without thinking. After all, a soldier doesn't march along on his head. All he needs are his legs. Marching, marching, marching, day and night. Left turn, right turn, left wheel, halt, by the right, quick march! Chest out, swing your arms! Fingers together, knees up! And finally, all our boot heels have to hit the ground together, to make a single crunching sound. That's the really important thing, the crunch.

Almost as important as marching is shooting with a rifle. A soldier's rifle is his girlfriend. A soldier has to be able to do everything with it. Even in his sleep. Exactly like the loading instructions in the rulebook: "LOADING THE RIFLE. Open the pan. Take the bullet. Powder in the pan. Shut the frizzen." And so on and so forth.

Before long, I notice that common soldiers are not allowed to speak to an officer about any ordinary thing. Officers, after all, are not ordinary people with whom you can have a normal conversation.

So I continue to put off my complaint from one day to the next.

A sergeant asks us recruits if there's anyone among us who's good with horses. I have to laugh. It's the first time I've laughed since becoming a soldier. I like horses more than I like most people.

"I'll have you laughing on the other side of your face!" bellows the sergeant. But at least I'm allowed to stay in the stable and sleep with the horses.

So it turns out to be good for me that my farmer wasn't some poor ox farmer, but a wealthy horse farmer. Only a few of the recruits are good with horses, whereas I know quite a bit about grooming and feeding and riding.

But I'm not allowed to ride.

After a couple of weeks, we're almost done with the marching and rifle loading. I join the transport corps of the horse artillery and am responsible for hitching up a pair of horses to a cannon, and feeding and brushing them. That's what I call proper work again. I like my horses, and my horses like me. Life starts to look up. It might even be an improvement on being with my farmer.

You can spot the soldiers from the horse artillery a long way off. They all wear the sky blue uniforms. Their civilian clothes have to be sent home. I've got my Sunday tunic in a corner of the stable. Where should I send it? I leave it hidden under the straw. I'm sure I'll need it again one day, when they find out I'm not really old enough to be a soldier.

After two more weeks, we have to pick up some new cannons. They say they were being molded and bored and filed in Ludwigsburg, day and night. The entire horse artillery squadron marches off, with the captain leading the way. The captain goes puce with pride when he sees those heavy bronze things. You can see it in his face and the way he struts about. The guns, brand-spanking-new, are glittering in the Christmas sun. Four six-pounders and two seven-pound howitzers. The captain is so beside himself with joy that he forgets himself for a moment. Proudly, he calls out to the soldiers that it won't be long before he uses the guns to shoot up Spain and Russia in the coming campaign.

So the cat's out of the bag. Something was in the offing. That's why the king needed all those soldiers and guns, they're all going to be used against Spain or Russia. To win. As always. Of course you win if you're on Napoleon's side. Napoleon is invincible. The whole world knows that.

Spain and Russia don't belong to Napoleon yet, but it's only a matter of time before they have to bow the knee to him, too. Someone mutters under his breath that Napoleon can never get enough of anything. He always needs more soldiers to play with and new battles to fight. We should mark his words, Russia won't be the end of it. Next will be India or some other place.

Foolishness? It's what all the little birdies are chattering from the barracks roofs. And if a little birdie says it, you have to take it seriously. Napoleon seems to be capable of anything.

5.

In the horse artillery there's a certain Sergeant Krauter. He doesn't like me. Why? No one knows. Not even I know. He bullies me any chance he gets. And as a sergeant, he has lots of opportunities. He makes me march through puddles till I look like one myself, and my leg muscles are quaking, and my sky blue uniform has turned dirt brown. But Sergeant Krauter only does that when there are puddles in the yard. Otherwise I have to go around collecting the balls of horse dung that are lying on the barracks yard, pick them up one by one with my fingers, march over to a wagon, and drop them there. And keep count of how many I've taken. Passing officers shake their heads when they see me, but they don't say anything, and they don't intervene. After all, what do they care about a private in the supply column and, in any case, they shouldn't undermine the authority of a sergeant.

Four hundred and seventy-eight dung balls in an hour.

I've had enough. No more. I want to run away. Deserting, they call it. Deserting is a very grave crime. You get shot for desertion, if they catch you. And almost all deserters do get caught. Most of them get caught within a few hours, the rest over time. Even so, I want to desert. I don't care. Because this is no sort of life, with the puddles and the dung balls. Just lately, Krauter threatened he would make me eat the dung balls.

I've got my Sunday tunic hidden under the straw. The next dark night, I'm going to change into it and run away from the barracks. Run off home to my farmer. He can explain everything. No matter what, I have to get away from Krauter and the dung balls.

Pitch-black night. The soldiers are snoring, and the horses are, too. Maybe the men are dreaming of women, and the horses of sacks of oats or something like that.

Tonight's the night. I've already pulled on my Sunday tunic and stashed the uniform in a corner.

Suddenly, the alarm is raised. Excited blowing of trumpets, swearing of oaths, running around, and the sergeant screaming at us to get out of the straw. Is it on account of me? No, it's not. I'm still here. I scramble back into my sky blue uniform and shove the Sunday tunic into the corner again.

Apparently, three men from the horse artillery had the same idea as me and ran away. A little before me. Took advantage of the dark and the fog to get over the barracks wall. Barely half an hour later, they've all been caught. They didn't realize that the whole town is like one big barracks, and that it's not so easy to get clear of it.

The deserting artillerymen aren't shot. Instead, they're condemned to running the gauntlet, which is worse than the firing squad, and usually just as fatal. The culprit ends up whipped to death. Apparently, the king has banned the practice. Says someone. But the generals like it. Because it's such a powerful deterrent. So no one heeds the king's decision. But then, maybe the king wasn't completely serious about it himself.

The drummer boy stands in the middle of the barracks yard. The dull thumps bounce off the walls like distant thunder. The whole barracks is standing there. Everyone wants to watch the deserters being punished and beaten to death by their comrades. Bets are being made on how far this man or that is going to get.

On the sandy ground of the barracks yard, the men of the horse artillery form up in a long double row. The captain takes charge personally. He makes a big speech about military honor. Whoever violates the terms of this honor should be beaten to death like a rabid dog.

"Anyone found not to strike with all his strength,"

the captain threatens us, "will be made to run the gauntlet himself!" Instead of twigs, the soldiers take the belts and harness from their uniforms and hold them ready over their shoulders.

The time is at hand. The three deserters are produced. One of them is very young. Almost a baby face. His eyes are wet. Fear twitches in his cheeks. In a few minutes, his short life will be over. He will lie broken on the sand and die.

They have to strip.

The first of them is driven between the rows. The belts and harnesses whistle down on his bare skin. He plunges like a maniac through the whistling belts. His comrades whip him mercilessly. No compassion. The captain watches every blow. The man stumbles on. He hurls himself through the gap between the soldiers. Head, back, and belly are bleeding.

My head is reeling. I can't see anything. It's as though I'm in a thick fog. The deserter is coming closer. I can hear his whistling breath. Did he just look at me reproachfully? He flings himself farther, under the lashing leather. He's made it! No, at the last moment he stumbles. The man next to the end put out a foot and tripped him. But he picks himself up and reaches the end of the alley. And so wins back his own life.

The young baby face doesn't get as far as me. He's left

on the floor halfway down. The last of them makes it about three-fourths of the way. He's stopped moving. Even so, his comrades continue to thrash him.

So two of them are done for. Beaten to death by their comrades. That's why they don't rate a Christian burial. Holes are dug for them among the suicides, against the cemetery wall. They're put in the ground in the middle of the night. Without any drums or ceremony. That's what everybody tells each other later on, in the collection depot. It's no great loss. Soldiers aren't worth much, and deserters aren't worth anything. It's wrong that one of them came out of it alive. Doesn't usually happen. Deserters deserve to die, simple as that. What sort of army would that be, if soldiers were just allowed to clear off any time they felt like it? How would kings and emperors fight their wars?

6.

So in the end, I'd rather stay where I am, with the soldiers. If desertion carries such grim consequences. Maybe I'll try it some other time. When things look more promising. Or maybe there'll be a miracle, and Sergeant Krauter will be told by the Almighty to bite the dust. So that I can get some peace and quiet.

But for the time being, he continues to bully me.

My sky blue uniform will never be clean again.

"Private Bayh is a disgrace!" the sergeant yells any chance he gets. "It appears he must wallow around in the mud like a sow."

And I can't get the smell of horse dung off my hands.

Then all at once, everything seems to take a turn to the better. Maybe fortune has an occasional attack of vertigo, or just a fit of hiccups.

On one particularly stinking day, I march past a

young lieutenant just as he's crossing the barracks yard. Because a lieutenant doesn't give ground to a private, he only barely scrapes past me. It's not my fault that he barely scrapes past me, because I've just been ordered by Sergeant Krauter to march smack through the biggest puddle in the yard. So it's no wonder that the white pants of the lieutenant catch several streaks of dirt. He looks down at them and becomes enraged.

"Hey!" he yells. "What do you think you are doing, soldier?"

But I am under orders from the sergeant, so I can't pay any special attention to the officer. I carry on marching through the big puddle. After all, I never had any orders to stop.

The sergeant sees what happened, and he tries to make himself scarce. But the lieutenant, who is steaming mad by now, grabs him by the lapels and makes him stand to attention.

"What do you think you're playing at, getting that fellow to spray me with dirt? Do you have any idea who's talking to you, man?"

The sergeant goes yellow and bumpy like an old plucked fowl.

"I'm afraid I didn't see you coming, sir!"

"What do you mean, you didn't see me? And what are you doing, keeping that boy tramping through puddles hour after hour?" the lieutenant asks indignantly.

I like hearing this, so to make sure I don't miss anything, I carry on marching on the spot. Of course the sergeant doesn't admit he's only bullying me for the devilish pleasure of it, because he enjoys having another human being in his power. No, of course he doesn't tell the lieutenant anything about his evil pleasure in my misery. "Purely a pedagogical measure, sir," he reports. "Transport soldier Bayh is a mulish individual, and, as if that weren't enough, he's as thick as two short planks. The least I want to do is get him to respond when he hears his own name."

Suddenly, the lieutenant commands: "Hold! Enough." He must mean me. I don't see anyone else marching. Then he orders, "Come over here." Of course, I obey immediately.

"So he's thick, is he?" the lieutenant asks the sergeant. "Really thick?"

"Even thicker than that! Your Grace, he's a moron."

The lieutenant looks me up and down.

I'm so dirty, I can hardly see out of my eyes. I feel as ashamed as a naked man in church. From top to bottom I'm spattered with barracks mud.

"What's your name?"

"Adam Feu . . . no! Georg Bayh," I stumble. It always happens like that, when I'm asked unexpectedly. I just can't get used to my name being Bayh.

What will the officer think of me? That I'm as thick

as they say? He looks like a decent fellow, the lieutenant. He can't be that old. His voice wobbles around as if it hasn't completely broken. He seems to have the same trouble I do. He has to be careful his voice doesn't crack, because the others will make faces and grin at him. Very annoying. I wonder how old the lieutenant can be? Soldiers are supposed to be eighteen and over. Not less. After all, they don't want children in the army. Except for me. But that's a different story. In my case, it's a mistake. With a lieutenant, it can be quite a normal state of affairs. There are apparently quite a lot of lieutenants who are seventeen. An aristocrat who goes to cadet school at the age of ten can well be a lieutenant by the time he's seventeen.

Not long ago, a sergeant was telling us how he knew a nobleman who had family all over the world. All his male relatives were with the army. He had an uncle who was a colonel with the Prussians, a brother who was a captain of horse with the Austrians, a cousin with the English redcoats, one who was a general for the czar, and one with the Turkish sultan. The whole clan knew and supported one another. That's why even the dimmest nobles get somewhere. At least in the army.

The lieutenant takes a long and thorough look at me.

"Well, now! What's your real name? Are you Adam Feu or Georg Bayh?" he suddenly asks.

The sergeant thrusts himself forward.

"Your Grace can see for himself. The boy is so stupid he doesn't even know his name. He's a real idiot, I say."

"Will you keep your opinions to yourself, unless I happen to ask you for them!" the officer snarls at him. Next he orders me to get myself cleaned up, and then go and report to him, Lieutenant Count Lammersdorf, in the officers' building. There, I'm going to have to get to work on his pants.

The lieutenant turns to the sergeant, who's standing there, frozen like a statue. "So you reckon transport soldier Bayh or Feu or whatever his name is, is really stupid?"

"Absolutely, sir," barks back the sergeant dutifully.

Another lieutenant comes by, stops, and looks at me, the filthy transport soldier. The two officers seem to be acquainted. "Here's a possibility," says the first lieutenant to the second, reflectively, without looking at me or the sergeant. "I need a replacement for my servant. He's such an incorrigible gossip. Where does that get us, if an officer's servant passes on everything he sees and hears in the mess? An officer's servant has to keep his lip buttoned."

"Well?" asks the second lieutenant. "And what's that got to do with this dirty specimen here?"

"This young fellow has certain advantages," says the first lieutenant. "It seems he's so thick he doesn't even know his own name. And there's no better servant for an officer than a fool. Plus I have a feeling that once he's been properly cleaned up and dressed, he'll actually look quite presentable." The two lieutenants smile to themselves at the same time.

"What do you think?" he asks.

"Cat's mess and trouser dung," says the other. "If he's as stupid as that, he won't even understand what we are talking about. And if he does understand anything, he won't understand it properly. He doesn't need to be clever to be able to brush and polish. You can do that with a small brain. And if there's something he doesn't know how to do, he'll probably be able to pick it up eventually."

"Exactly!" crows the first lieutenant, and then he hisses in the sergeant's face: "And this has nothing to do with you, by the way."

"No, sir! Nothing to do with me," affirms the sergeant.

Neither the one nor the other nor the third of them says a word to me, and of course none of them asks me what I think. I really didn't know how stupid I was. But in the army, all things are possible. You can't be surprised by anything.

And so it comes that I have to leave my lodgings with the horses and move into a little room in the officers' quarters. I can't say I'm overjoyed. I'd much rather be with horses than some wellborn officer. I know I can get on with horses, but a titled officer is another matter. But maybe I'll learn. The way I once learned with horses.

I'm living with the lieutenant now. After a couple of days, it dawns on me that an officer is only human as well. Sometimes my noble master has nothing noble about him. If there's no one watching him, he can behave just like a stable boy. But I like that in him.

My new work isn't so bad. I only need to work like half a farmhand. Or even less. I don't have anything to do with my lieutenant's food. The officers always mess together. They've got their own cook, or even two cooks, so that they don't have to eat as commonly as the common troops. In the morning I wake my gentleman. I brush his lieutenant's coats, and in the evenings, I pull the boots off his feet, polish them to a mirroring shine, wash his pants and socks, run errands for him, and I don't know what else. My new service is bearable, easy, and good. No more backbreaking labor. No stable cleaning, no heavy wheelbarrow loads to be trundled onto the dung heap. And every little detail is explained to me. Whatever I haven't expressly been told to do, I can leave undone. Does the lieutenant really take me for so stupid that he has to tell me everything? As if I had nothing but straw between my ears? Never mind. What's much more important is that Sergeant Krauter doesn't have me in his power anymore. Because a lieutenant is far senior and has much more authority than a sergeant.

The lieutenant owns a couple of racehorses. Beautiful creatures. Purebred Arabs. But he won't let me near them. Is that on account of my stupidity, too? He's brought his own stable boy along from home. I'm jealous.

My room is tiny, but I have it all to myself. My bed, too. Never in my life have I had my own room. What more could I want? It's a big step forward. All at once, I feel proper and distinguished. In fact, I feel much better off here than I was with my farmer.

What about my officer? He's very young and very spoiled. I bet he's never had to muck out a stable or castrate a tomcat with a couple of stones. But in spite of that, he's still a decent sort, even if there's something half done about him. He's halfway between mother's milk and rum punch, as the old folks would say. But the officer's saber and the epaulettes, they give him a lot of authority.

I'm completely satisfied with my new life. I have enough to eat, I have a roof over my head, no fleas or lice, and a uniform that fits. I had to trade in the sky blue gear, which I couldn't get clean anymore anyway, for a green uniform. I'm no longer part of the horse artillery, but with the mounted Jagers, like my noble lieutenant.

And suddenly it's not just that I may ride, I have to. That's how quickly life sometimes changes. I have no trouble with the riding. After all, I sat up on horseback even when I was a little boy, bareback. A saddle makes things even easier. It fits your bottom like a glove.

My lieutenant didn't want to be attended by some kind of scarecrow, so he took the trouble to come along when I was being kitted out. He saw to it that the seat of my new pants doesn't hang down to the back of my knees. So everything's shipshape. Well, everything would be, if only the lieutenant would treat me like a normal human being. Which he won't. He treats me like a little snot nose, or a person with a shrunken or underdeveloped brain.

It's enough to make you despair. Am I really such a useless dimwit?

Maybe it's not the lieutenant's fault. Maybe all the noble gentlemen are like that and see in the rest of humanity only fools to give orders to.

Every evening, the wellborn gentlemen pay calls on

one another. Sometimes they meet at one officer's place, sometimes another's. Sometimes they collect at my lieutenant's. Then I have to serve wine and pear brandy and run around topping up glasses. It can go on half the night. Usually, it ends around midnight because there are a couple of elderly gents in the officers' building who can't drink as much as they'd like, and who need sleep on account of their years. The young lieutenants, though, they can put away wine by the liter, and they smoke their smelly pipes like Croats and talk all sorts of nonsense. At first, it sounded very clever to me, but before long I realized that it was all empty talk. It's just as well if I forget it as soon as I've heard it.

Sometimes the gentlemen speak in French. That sounds better behaved and cleverer because I really haven't the foggiest what they're talking about. And they laugh as wildly as the head stable boy used to do when he patted the maid on the behind or pushed his hand up her skirts. The more wine the officers drink, the more stupid stuff they talk. Almost every time, I have to clear away someone's puke. Most of the lieutenants, it seems, can't judge how much wine they can pour into themselves before they start to overflow.

After these parties, my lieutenant usually lies in bed pretty wrecked and as pale and white as his nightshirt. He's as whipped as a little doggie. It's not a good time for him or me. He is in such a bad way, he has trouble keeping up his aristocratic manners. In the end, he even starts whimpering and sobbing to break your heart and calling for his mama. It's as if his usual common sense is blotted out by weeds or dung heaps, and his soul has a lot of mess to deal with. When he's at that stage, I can't leave him on his own. I have to sit by his bed, hold the bucket ready, and talk to him about anything, just to try and calm him down. Tell him stories I heard from the hands and maids of my farmer, or others that happened to me. Or else I mix up all sorts of possible and impossible things. The way the old people do with their fairy tales. I expect the lieutenant is used to that from his mother or his nurse or some governess or other. Usually, he falls asleep while I'm talking to him. Sleep purifies body and soul and brings them back into balance somehow. Till the next time, anyway.

8.

It's a warmish evening, one of the last days in February. The first coltsfoot flower is blooming on the sunniest spot in the barracks yard. Of course, one coltsfoot doesn't mean it's spring. But it's the first hint that it's on its way.

There's a feeling of unrest in the reception depot. The officers' building is like a chicken coop. Doors swinging, the gentlemen dashing in and out.

My lieutenant's cheeks are flushed with excitement too.

"At last we're going to see some action," he says, like some first-grader who can't wait to get to school. "Pack everything ready as for field march!" he orders me. "Tomorrow morning we're moving out."

War? Even so, I'm pleased. At last I'm going to get out and see a bit of the world. I have no idea what war is like. I've never been in one, and I only know from hearsay that it's when soldiers hack and stab and shoot at one another. And if you happen to be there yourself, you have to try and make sure that the bullets fly past you, and that the sabers and lances miss when they hack and stab. War makes heroes. Who are generally dead by the time it's over. Except for the generals. They can become heroes without dying first.

The lieutenant's squire suddenly comes down with something. The prospect of war probably gave him the runs. He's no soldier after all, he's just a squire. Why should he go to war? So I get his riding horse. And because a lieutenant count takes care of mounting and dismounting and riding, but quite naturally not feeding and currycombing, I suddenly find myself in charge of three horses, instead of just one.

"Look after them carefully," the lieutenant says anxiously. And then he adds, in a funny squeaky voice, "I swear by the sun, the moon, and the stars, I'll chop you up into little tiny pieces if anything happens to the horses."

But he doesn't have to worry. I like horses best of all living creatures anyway.

The mounted Jager regiment leaves the barracks in the morning at the prescribed time, and crosses the Neckar about an hour later. On the other side is a little village with a church and low farmhouses. The whole village quakes and trembles as the glittering, thundering troops make their way through on the narrow dirt road.

I'm pretty pleased to belong to such a magnificent regiment. And to go to war as part of it. War can't be so bad. We'll just ride everything down. On my splendid Arab and with this glittering army, war can only be a beautiful thing.

Where the war is going to be, though, no one is quite sure.

Down in Spain, says someone. It's supposed to be warm there all the time. And the girls are the most beautiful in the world. Dark and proud and crisp as honey cakes.

In the east, say others. In Russia! Where else? The whole world knows Napoleon wants to conquer Russia. Russia's not so good. It's cold there, and the girls aren't half so beautiful, but heavy and dumpy.

Apparently, the crown prince is with the army. But he's not traveling with our regiment. He's taking some other route.

If the king sends his son along, then the war's in the bag. With an army like ours, and with the invincible Napoleon at the helm.

Maybe I'll be lucky enough to clap eyes on the greatest general in history for myself.

The February sun is getting warmer and more pleasant. The regiments trot and march across the country at a comfortable pace. The wheels of the cannon and the many baggage and forage carts rut the big roads. Slowly the giant worm of the army winds its way forward. No need to hurry. The strength of horses and men must be conserved for the encounter with the enemy. And the reserves mustn't fall too far behind.

A town appears on the horizon. The regiment rides past it. It's the town where my farmer left me just three months ago. I don't want to think about it.

The regiment stops for the night in a valley. The villages fill up with soldiers from the mounted Jägers. As befits a count, my lieutenant is put up in the castle. Turns out he's related to the master of the castle. Are there any nobles to whom he *isn't* related? I trot along after him, to discharge my duties as his officer's servant. Of course, I'm not quartered in the castle. That wouldn't be right, and, anyway, I have my place with the horses. The stable is roomy. Most of the officers' horses and servants end up in there. The horses are given beets, hay, and oats, and the servants plenty of bread and pear juice. I pull off my uniform, burrow down into the hay next to my horses, and sleep contentedly as any weary wanderer who has reached his destination. The war is getting off on the right foot.

Only rarely do I spare a thought for my farmer, his big cow shed, and his vast dung heap.

9.

Usually it's like this: You think you've made it into heaven, and suddenly you drop out of the clouds into the deepest pile of dreck.

It must be the end of February. That's when the thing with heaven and dreck happens to me.

The day doesn't begin badly. I feed the horses. Then I currycomb them till they whinny with rapture. It makes me happy when my lieutenant is happy, and it makes him happy when his horses are happy. When they stand there all glossy and healthy.

I wait outside the castle for a window to open. Then I'll know that my master needs me. He can't get into his boots alone, and he has trouble with his tight pants as well.

An hour later, the lieutenant is suddenly standing in front of me so sheepish and uncertain, as if he'd gone in his pants. He can't look into my eyes, and he tells me in a wobbling, squeaky voice that his father has sent out two replacements for the stable boy who was sent home sick. They are both trusty servants of long years' standing, but also experienced soldiers, who now must go to war with the lieutenant. And look after him. On orders of the old count. Everything's been sorted out with the colonel. As is the way among titled gentlemen.

All of which makes me rapidly surplus to requirements. From one moment to the next. His Grace the lieutenant is very sorry. I see he means it. But he can't use me anymore. Three servants is too many for him. The colonel wouldn't stand for it.

I am stunned.

I walk away.

And so I fall out of heaven into the middle of the muck. The muck is back at the other end of the regiment. I am quartered on a spill of straw next to a dung pile and a horse. The billet is poor, and the horse is worse. An awful animal. That's how it goes, apparently. Last come gets the lousiest horse. A beast no one else would look at. In the other corner, to make things worse, are a couple of men from the Jagers. Their glee is written all over their faces. One of them must have seen me once riding the noble Arab. Now he congratulates me on this new mount. "It's without exception the rottenest nag, the most ill-tempered monster in the regiment. The devil himself must have created that animal in a fit of rage or delirium."

But that's not enough to cause the world to end, I think. Anyway, wisdom comes with time, and I shouldn't be dissatisfied, because things could have been worse. The horse looks me up and down, a little sadly, but not maliciously. So, for all its ugliness it does have a good nature. I will try to make friends with it, be strict but considerate, and then it will be the devil's work if I can't cope with it. At least I'll make an effort. It's got to work. Not least on account of the nasty faces around me. Once again, the horse shoots me a not unfriendly look. I stroke it cautiously. It doesn't resist. Well, there's a start. After all, a horse isn't a person, and so it could never be half as malicious.

By the next day, the horse is obeying me. It doesn't mind me sitting on it. I'm really proud of myself, and the horsemen around me are suddenly full of respect, and don't tease me anymore.

But it's too early to draw breath. My plunge has hardly begun.

The mounted Jagers don't want to keep me. The regiment can't have a man over, all of a sudden. Too few, yes, that happens all the time. But not one over. That's never happened. The Jagers remember where they got me from, and they make inquiries. Yes, of course, we're missing transport corps soldier Bayh, the horse artillery says. A certain Sergeant Krauter is missing me badly. So badly that the Russian war cannot be won without me. The guns need me. Desperately.

I could tear myself to pieces with rage and fear. The battery is in the next village. I have to walk. A long walk. Should I make a break for it? Not possible, in the green uniform. A child could tell from a mile off that I'm a mounted Jager, and not some peasant. I'd have to run naked. Can't do that, either. Partly from shame, and partly because it's still too cold.

Sergeant Krauter takes immediate receipt of me. His glee comes puffing out of both nostrils. He admires my pretty green uniform. With a smile, he promises me that he'll have it as brown as dung in the space of a few days. As brown as my last blue one had been. "Inside and out," he promises me with a sneer.

Now I'm back in the transport corps, in charge of two huge horses, and responsible for getting them harnessed up with others to the heavy seven-pound howitzers. The sergeant torments me every chance he gets, and he makes up for everything he missed during my absence. Because it's war and he can't keep me marching through puddles, he's had a few new ideas. For instance, he makes me walk along behind the seven-pound gun, always just me. "You're responsible for seeing nothing gets lost!" Because I don't get enough sleep, I stumble along in the wake of the cannon. No sooner has the horse artillery reached the day's destination after a long march than I am sent out on sentry duty. It's no wonder I'm so tired, the spoon falls from my hand. While the others are asleep, I stagger along reeling with exhaustion among the cannons and the horses. And in between I polish the bronze cannons. At all times of day and night I am ordered to wipe them down. I have a feeling I scrub them so much, they're getting smaller.

The war isn't what it was. Krauter's gone and spoiled it. As if I didn't have enough to worry about, my toes are bleeding into my boots. One morning my good boots that fit me weren't there. In their place, two downtrodden foot holders. When I wear them, I slither around and my toes and heels keep hitting their tough edges.

Who stole my boots? Who would do such a thing? The sergeant? What sort of war is it where your enemy isn't any Russian, but the sergeant of your own company?

By now, it must have gotten to be March. More and more men and horses are streaming up out of the south. We all congregate in the Hohenlohe. Marching troops, splendid horsemen on light and heavy horses, guns and wagons. And the magnificent uniforms! In every color, blue and green and yellow and red. I'm sure God is happy. He can see the colorful royal army going by at His feet, as beautiful as a flowery meadow.

My feet, though, are bloody.

One dull morning, the Wurttemburg regiments are drawn up on parade. There's a large castle in the mist. "It belongs to the count of Hohenlohe!" someone says. Everyone gets to polishing and brushing and currycombing. Is it a battle coming? No, of course not. Before a battle, you don't brush up cannons, and anyway, we're still in our own country. It's a long way yet to Russia. Hundred times as far. It's bound to be a thousand miles and more.

Then the rumor goes like wildfire through the regiments.

"The king's coming!"

"He wants to bid his soldiers good luck as they leave the country."

"What a good king!"

In a long, broad field he's standing with his crown prince and various generals and people from the court. All of them mounted, naturally. To make them look powerful and important. The regiments gallop past. It's the first time I don't have to march. I'm allowed to sit up next to the cannon. The heavy howitzers skip fast over the uneven turf. The king doesn't have much time. Apparently. He wants to see all his men as they move out to war and say good-bye to them.

I don't see much myself. Really just the powerful horse on which the king is sitting. What a big beast. A heavy special order from nature. The king needs it, too. So there's enough space for his hanging guts, and so his weight doesn't crush the horse.

The whole hullabaloo is over quickly.

Afterward there's a lot of talk about it. Secretly of course, and so quietly you can hear next to nothing. So the wrong person doesn't see or hear anything. The nice-looking young man with the fat king is apparently his bosom friend, a Count Dillen.

I wonder what a bosom friend is? Something quite special, I'll be bound, because the gallant had a general's uniform on and a splendid spirited horse under him. The sergeants and sergeant majors grin subtly. Maybe they're just disrespectful, or else they know something I don't know.

Are you allowed to grin like that about His Majesty, the highest of the high, the king? Without immediate punishment from Heaven?

10.

The following morning, the regiments move off. We carry on in a northerly direction, toward Franconia. I'd never heard of Franconia before. It's a pity that the only foreign land they taught us about at school was the Holy Land. It was probably the only one the teacher knew about.

There's supposed to be a royal military paymaster somewhere, the chancellor with a big chest full of money. But where is he? Somewhere behind us? He hasn't yet got as far forward as us, at any rate. So there's no wages. And no wine. But the officers always have money. They can go out and get soused every night. If that's what they want. Mostly, they do. After all, who knows how much longer they're going to remain alive?

A soldier's life is a merry life. For the officers, anyway.

Sergeant Krauter doesn't have any money, but still he drinks wine. He secretly sells off the harness of one of the draft horses. Afterward, he gives me the blame for its disappearance. I was asleep on sentry duty, and the next day the stuff was gone, the harness. Everyone believes the sergeant, no one believes me. After all, he carries a saber and I don't. Krauter doesn't seem to be bothered by any sort of conscience. If I had my way, I'd shoot him at the moon with one of the seven-pound howitzers. Now I won't get a red cent in wages, for months. Until the harness has been paid for.

What a dog's life! If only the war with the Russians would start soon. So there's an end to this marching, and Sergeant Krauter has something else to think about other than tormenting me.

Our regiment continues to advance through the beautiful land of Franconia. Such rich country. No little handkerchief fields and stony ground, like we have at home. Everything rich and bountiful. I wish I could take a little pleasure in it myself.

There's something else I wish for. The sergeant. That bastard. I wish I was shot of him. It should be like the fairy tale my father told me long ago, when I was very little. In it, there was a farmer who had three wishes. I wouldn't even need three wishes. Just one would be enough for me. What would I use it for? I wouldn't even need time to think. Sergeant Krauter to fall off his horse. Drunk, as he always is. He wouldn't have to break his neck. His arms and legs would be fine by me. I just want him to be invalided out, unfit for service.

These sort of un-Christian thoughts mob my head. I spend the whole day latched on to one of these fantasies. It's all I think about. Just the busted sergeant. When I'm anywhere near him, I stare at him very hard. My head feels as though it might burst, that's how hard I'm concentrating on him.

"Knock Sergeant Krauter off his horse!" I beseech some dark powers.

But the sergeant sits firmly in his saddle and continues to tyrannize me.

In the afternoon, though, I almost succeed. In the distance lies the fortress of Coburg. A wonderful, fairy-tale castle. How beautiful the world is, after all! Or rather, would be, I think. If the sergeant left me in peace. Which he has no notion of doing. I can't stand it much longer. Before long, I'll have lost my personal war against him.

A terrible rage takes me. I make an enormous effort, and suddenly it happens.

"Sergeant!" I order him silently, but with supernatural force. "Slip out of your stirrup and fall off! I want a good fall, so you break your collarbone, or a couple of ribs at least." I wish so fervently that I feel the veins swell in my temples and start to hurt.

Maybe I happen to blink, or else the sergeant is too drunk — drunkards have a special guardian angel watching over them — or else it's a strange accident. Anyway, it isn't Sergeant Krauter who slips out of his stirrups, but the man beside him. He lurches to the side, and off he goes. And then the horse following goes and steps on him, too, which horses usually avoid doing. Nothing at all happens to the sergeant.

I made my supreme effort in vain. I'm only grateful no one realizes that I might be responsible for the accident. It doesn't even occur to Krauter. He doesn't suspect that I, transport soldier Bayh, may have such powers.

At any rate, I go on being tyrannized day and night. My curses on him get more and more vicious. But nothing happens anymore. I have no access to my devilish magic powers. Or they don't exist. I hope the war in Russia will be fairer, and Sergeant Krauter catches a cannonball in the bum.

There's still no war, though. Russia is so far away, it seems incredible that we could walk there. Perhaps the country doesn't really exist, and the whole army is just tramping about on some cooked-up whim of Napoleon's.

The army crawls into the Thuringian Forest. That marks the end of paradise. There is no more wine.

Instead, there's snow again, and an icy north wind that blows through our uniforms. Apparently, there are now difficulties with our supplies. The baggage column can't keep up with us. Already, with Russia and our foes still so far away. An old sergeant, who has already fought both with and against Napoleon, blasphemes, "What's it going to be like when we're in enemy country, in the endless plains of Russia?"

We have our first experience of hunger. A few men still have supplies.

I don't. And I continue to stumble and trudge along behind the seven-pound howitzer. My toenails have turned blue. I can barely walk. My bloody stumps of toes rub themselves raw with every step. Perhaps it'll help if I stuff some old leaves in my boots. No, that doesn't seem to make any difference. I need new boots. Desperately. Before my feet go to pot, and the rest of me along with them.

I start to keep an eye out on the various carts that are accompanying us. Before long, I figure out which one carries what. An army of this size has to drag all sorts of things with it. Including shoes and boots. I make a report and show my toes. "If we issued you new boots, now, where would that get us? And besides, there aren't any!" exclaims Sergeant Krauter. And because he's my immediate superior, and I have no one else to report to, I continue to trudge along in these deadly boots.

I am left with no alternative but to perpetrate a grave sin. At night, I steal. It's not especially difficult. No one's sleeping in the shoe cart. No one catches me. After all, I'm supposed to be the one apprehending any thieves. It's to my own advantage that I'm set to watch over myself. Cautiously, I creep into the cart and help myself to a pair of well-made boots that fit. Here's the odd thing — I don't feel at all guilty. Even though I've robbed His Very Highness, the king.

So that my new footwear won't draw too much attention to itself, I rub and scratch the new leather and smear dirt onto the boots till they look run-down and awful. Like my old ones. Now I can keep up with the column. My toes and heels calm down, the bleeding stops, and they're on the way to being cured by the time the horse artillery leaves the kingdom of Saxony behind. My two big toenails start to work loose. Later on, past Smolensk, they both drop off. But I'm young, so it's no great matter. Under the purplish scales of the old nails, healthy new ones are already starting to grow.

No one notices that I've got these brand-new boots in place of my old ones. For a while, I continue to hobble like a cripple behind the shiny howitzer, just so Sergeant Krauter doesn't get any stupid ideas.

II.

In April, the Wurttemburg regiments are in the Leipzig area. There are no enemy Russians here, either. The enemy's still at least a thousand miles off, so says Sergeant Krauter. Maybe he's right, too, because a sergeant is bound to know more about maps and terrain than an ordinary transport soldier. If I hem and haw about it all in my mind, I don't really know what to think. Why doesn't Napoleon find himself an enemy who's a little closer at hand? But they say he's already used them all up.

In any case, there's still no sign of a real war. Except for the terrible Krauter. It's just as well, too, as far as the Wurttemburg army is concerned, because we have our hands full with our own problems. Food and fodder are becoming scarce.

Fortune and misfortune are still in the balance with me.

One evening, my former lieutenant comes galloping along on his lovely Arab steed, into the little Saxon village where the gleaming seven-pound howitzers and horses and Krauter and a few transport soldiers and I are bivouacked. His other horse is cantering at his side. He is in a towering rage.

The cause is the two noble servants sent by his father. The ones who caused me to tumble from heaven straight into the clutches of Sergeant Krauter only weeks ago. Now they help me get out of my pickle. Not directly, because the two of them probably don't know who I am, and they're miles away in any case. Gone. A clean pair of heels. They seem to have had enough of this war and don't want to accompany Napoleon to Russia. Somewhere in the area of Leipzig, they left their noble master in the lurch, most shamefully. A right pair of dogs.

So the lieutenant wants me back. Just like that.

The captain of the cannoneers is produced. Then he and Sergeant Krauter are hissing and trembling with fury. They protest so noisily, with hands and feet, that the lieutenant count stands his Arab menacingly on its hind legs. But never mind what fuss the two of them try to make, none of it's the least use. Because the lieutenant has in his hand a piece of paper issued by the colonel, allowing him to take the soldier Georg Bayh just like that, without further ado. As his servant. After all, a lieutenant count can't very well go to war without a servant, especially a war that's supposed to take place as far away as Russia seems to be.

Half an hour later, I'm mounted on the second of the splendid Arabs, riding away with my old and new master under the astonished glances of the cannoneers. It's nothing to do with me, because naturally no one asks me for my preference. Where would that get us anyway, if a common soldier had to be asked whether he's in agreement with an order or not?

So I'm able to escape Sergeant Krauter for a second time. I hope for good! Of course, I'm very happy to obey. In fact, I'm so delighted that I feel like flinging myself around the neck of my lieutenant. But I look completely unmoved, just like a good soldier should.

Straight afterward, another extraordinary thing happens. A farmer's wife secretly slips me a hunk of bread with roast meat. Me. Not my master. How good people can be, after all! At least, some of them.

I wonder if I should share it with my lieutenant. Why should I? On the one hand, he got me out of the clutches of the sergeant, but on the other hand, the farmer's wife meant her gift for me. So I eat it all by myself. But I don't feel happy doing it. I'm sure my lieutenant is hungry, and I feel selfish and greedy.

Now I'm charged with currycombing the noble horses again and finding fodder for them. I try to provide for myself and for His Grace, the lieutenant, as well. At the moment, there's no cook for the officers. Either he's stuck in the dust, miles back with his kitchen equipment, or else he's hightailed it, taken his supplies with him, and sold them off.

Finding food isn't an easy matter. There's nothing to be had far and wide, and the many regiments eat the country bare like a million-strong rat pack. There isn't even anything to be had with money. Often, stealing is the only thing left to do. After all, I have to keep my lieutenant and me alive.

Every week, I wash his dirty pants and socks. My own as well. But separately. It wouldn't do to have my things and His Grace's muddled up while laundering them. Probably on account of the different qualities of dirt. My pants need to dry overnight. In the morning, when I creep out of the hay, I pull them on. I have only the one pair.

The many regiments are making slow progress at the moment. More are joining us all the time. From every side. My lieutenant tells another lieutenant that not in all the history of the world have there been so many soldiers assembled in one place. But then there has never been another Napoleon, either.

So here we have half a million men making their way to Russia, and — as if it were the main street of the village at home — I walk slap-bang into someone I know. Our cavalry is just passing an infantry regiment on the banks of the Elbe. People call out here and there. I know the accent. So these must be Wurttemburgers. I'm pleased to see them. The poor foot sloggers are shuffling along apathetically in completely done-in boots. I feel so lucky to have landed with the mounted Jagers. There are worse things than being saddle sore.

"Hey, you!" calls one of the foot sloggers. "Aren't you our mayor's farmhand?"

I'm startled, and ask my lieutenant for permission to hang back a little, because there's someone from my village among the infantry. I wouldn't mind stopping and having a chat with him.

I walk alongside the foot soldiers for a good long while, leading my horse by the reins. The soldier is Hanselmann, the son of the village cobbler, and he's got plenty of news for me. There's another fellow in the regiment who hails from the same village, and he's just back from a visit there. Everything in the village is fine. My farmer has taken on a new farmhand. So he doesn't seem to be counting on my return anymore. The farmer's wife is on her deathbed. Sad for her! *Ach,* life is hard. I hear more news. Nothing particular, but the little village weighs heavy on my soul afterward.

The lieutenant has stopped treating me like a snot

nose. Somewhere he seems to have noticed that I can think a little bit. I get a new uniform again. The old one never recovered from Sergeant Krauter's efforts. My well-born master obtains everything he wants, so of course that includes a fresh uniform for me, as his servant. There's only one thing he can't seem to get, and that's enough food for his horses, himself, and me. The world around us seems to have been eaten bare. Only hunger is so plentiful that it hurts.

It's something like the middle of April. One evening, the regiment emerges onto a wide plain. In the distance, we make out a large town on a big river. "Frankfurt and the Oder," says my lieutenant. Not to me, of course, but to the squadron leader, who's riding along at his side. This Frankfurt place seems incredibly far from home. I wonder if we'll ever make it back? I hope Napoleon knows his way around.

The infantry marches into town with fifes and drums. We can hear the stamp of thousands of boots on the paving stones. The cavalry regiments, as ever, are told to take a roundabout route through the outlying villages. Because of the many horses, which would stink up the city in no time.

It's a lovely spring with beautiful meadows and fresh-looking green forests. In the farm orchards and on the roadsides there is the snow white of sloe and cherry blossoms. The occasional pear tree even tries to bloom. The grass is full of masses of bright yellow dandelions.

Our column rides across the country nine or ten hours a day. The weather is perfect. I have stopped thinking about my sore feet. They are healing well and hurt less and less. Instead, I have trouble with my behind. But that's getting accustomed to whole days in the saddle. Perhaps it's turning into leather too. Not my pants, though; they are getting thinner. The lieutenant has more trouble with his bottom. Apparently, his noble skin is finer and more delicate. At the end of hours of riding, he has to stand up in the stirrups for relief. In the evening he slinks into the stable for me to pull off his boots and also to rub some salve that the regimental doctor has prescribed into his wellborn bottom.

12.

Blossom time is over, and the meadows have been mown. The air is full of the smell of new hay. The horses can eat to their hearts' content. There is nothing else, anyway. Only hay and water. In the long run, it's not good for them. There are no oats. Too many riders have already passed through in front of us. They and their horses have eaten up everything. In a few days, the hay will run out as well.

And the army is getting bigger all the time. Who ever saw so many soldiers? From the west, one regiment after another moves into line, Westphalians and Italians, Austrians, Bavarians, Portuguese, and more and more French. I am astonished by the number of Frenchmen. And boys, too. Poles come up from the south. They are especially colorful. They are also the only ones who seem to know what they are fighting for. They want to reclaim their country from the Russians. And what are the Wurttemburgers fighting for? For their greedy guts of a king? He's fat enough already, if you ask me.

Damn it all, I think. What is this gigantic army going to live off? So many horses and men. Enough to graze the whole country down to stubble. It can't go well. Eventually, they'll end up eating one another.

Where are the forage wagons with oats and hay and biscuits? From what we hear, they're miles back, sinking into the deep sand of the Polish roads. Another lieutenant tells my lieutenant count that the infantry regiments are making less and less progress. Their boots are useless, cheap rubbish that goes to pieces in no time. The king of Wurttemburg has the answer, smirks the other lieutenant. He has sent out fifty four-axled wagons, carrying ten thousand pairs of boots for his soldiers. And biscuits. From Stuttgart. The lieutenant whispers behind his hand, "And what if it's true? Even if it's true, the wagons will never get here. They're bound to bog down somewhere on the way, get looted, and have their contents flogged off!"

My conscience weighs on me. I stole boots, too, back then. I feel them burning on my feet. No, I convince myself, it wasn't theft, it was necessity. After all, this is war. Other laws apply.

In a little town in Poland, there's a huge procession.

With priests and banners and crowds and flowers. Someone says it's a Catholic-Popish celebration called Corpus Christi. They have something like that in Upper Wurttemburg, too. Some of the Bavarians and Austrians accompany the procession a ways. So we have Papists among us, too.

Today, the regiment requisitions for the first time. That's what people do in war. They just take the food and the fodder they need for themselves and their horses from the local people. Of course it's not theft as such, because it's war, and the people it's taken from are given a receipt for it. For that reason it's not called stealing, but requisitioning. The squadron leader says mockingly to the lieutenant that he wouldn't mind if the receipts were a bit bigger. Then at least people would have something to wipe their arses with.

My lieutenant has been put in charge of a forage unit. He has to requisition in a certain area. Cattle and sheep, as many as possible. And anything the horses will eat. Forage and food for three weeks. For the entire regiment. The unit is given three days. Then they have to be back. With food for the men and horses, of course. Otherwise, the regiment will starve. So the forage detail rides off into the Polish countryside on this Popish holiday, from place to place, and from farm to farm. But we don't find anything. The farmers and their animals have fled into the forests.

Eventually, we do encounter some people: old women and small children. They stand around looking terrified. Too many soldiers had already been there before us, the old women say. The soldiers took everything and left them to starve.

"Who cares!" hisses the lieutenant. "It's every man for himself, and besides, our regiment is part of the *Grande Armée*, which is to conquer Russia, and we can't do that without food."

Then the foraging troop catches the last chicken, looks through the woodshed, and finds a little sack of corn.

I look my lieutenant in the eye, and then I see that it's not easy for him to take the last bit of food away from these poor people.

What was this Napoleon thinking of? Every farrier knows that a horse needs to eat so-and-so much, and people need so-and-so much. Napoleon should have done his sums ahead of time, and then he would have understood what his *Grande Armée* could be expected to get through.

For hours, the forage troop rides tired and depressed through loose birch woods. The last rays of the sun touch the trunks and make them gleam. Lying amongst them are patches of sour grass and black swamp holes. Nothing but crippled little birch trees with stunted bilberries among their roots and long-withered heather tufts. Since early afternoon, the platoon hasn't encountered a single living soul. The world seems to be coming to an end here. The barrenness oppresses us. What are we doing here? There's nothing useful for us in this place. No hay, not a speck of corn, no eggs, no goats, let alone any oxen or milk cows. From time to time a rabbit bounds over the dry ground from one burrow to another. That would be a tasty morsel. Perhaps one mouthful. But the little animal is just taunting us. It won't let us catch it. It peeps out at us cheekily from its burrow, and if anyone makes a move toward it, it's gone. The detail doesn't have time to lie in wait for it or to dig up its underground tunnels.

I am tormented by a daydream or some sort of devilish notion. Each time I look around, I see a rider following us at a certain distance. That by itself wouldn't matter so much. But the pursuer has the features and the outline of Sergeant Krauter. Even though I know I can't recognize anyone for sure at such a distance, I am unable to shake off my anxiety.

I hope the lieutenant finds his way out of the swamp again.

By and by, the platoon could use somewhere to spend the night. But there isn't anywhere. For over an hour now, we've been on a narrow path winding over swampy ground. One pace to either side, and the swamp will swallow up man and horse.

We are a sorry column — supposed to bring back food and fodder for an entire regiment, and we're suffering from hunger ourselves. The path is getting ever narrower. Left and right of us, we hear the squelch and gurgle of swamp holes. Woe to anyone who steps in one of those! He won't need burying. Of course, it starts to get dark, as on every other day, and, as if to make matters worse, a mist rises. The path disappears in the murk. No sign of a farm anywhere. No light and no sound. We feel out the narrow path and sway across the swampy land. Suddenly, it's night through and through. The mist turns into a thick, impenetrable fog. No starlight can make its way through that soup. The lieutenant orders us to halt. Before someone makes a misstep and is gone for good.

Who has a torch? Or anything else flammable that we can use to light our way? Who thinks of such things ahead of time? The horses are getting restless. They can sense perdition half a step away. There is no possibility of resting or lying down. There is no place to sit or lie anywhere.

We must wait for morning. Thank God the nights are short at this time of year and not too cold.

The riders of the platoon are drawn up in a long line along the narrow path. Behind me, I hear someone snoring. The horses are cropping the thin, sour plants on the wayside. That's all there is. The lieutenant is tired as well. He's slumped over the neck of his noble Arab and keeps slipping off. I hold his horse on a long tether and take up a position directly behind the lieutenant. So that he doesn't fall off the path. Otherwise, he might sink in the bog. And if I happened to drop off as well, I wouldn't be able to pull him out. That means I have to stay awake. That's not too hard for me, because I feel this terrible grinding and churning in my belly. Even though there's nothing to grind. I've got nothing in there but some pond water. But maybe I failed to notice a few tadpoles and they're now swimming around. Anyway, I need to go, urgently. More urgently by the second. Of course, I can't very well squat down next to my lieutenant count. That wouldn't be right at all. On account of the respect I bear him, and the possible smell. So I crawl off a ways on all fours. Not in the swamp, please! I feel left and right with my hands. One side is dry. Still dry. Good! More dry! That way, I don't need to do it directly on the path, where everyone would see it in the morning when we rode on. Further to the right. Dry. No more ponds. I stand up and feel my way forward. Suddenly, the fog disappears. I've reached the edge of the swamp.

Happily, I wake the lieutenant. I am so relieved I grab him crudely by the arm and pull him out of his sleep.

"Hey, Your Nobleness!" I yell, against all the rules. "Wake up! The world is just a few yards that way."

For the first time, the lieutenant count touches me. He briefly lays his hand on my shoulder.

That same night, the forage troupe is riding across

endless pastures, among calves and sheep. They must have corn and oats and everything the regiment so badly needs. The lieutenant is already building castles in the air. We can take half the sheep and calves. If every rider manages to drive ten animals ahead of him, the regiment will have nothing to worry about.

A clear early summer morning dawns over this paradise. In front of us is a large farmstead with all the trimmings, a noble manor house complete with barns and cow sheds and simple abodes for the farmhands and the maids.

The lieutenant laughs, he really does. Not just a tight grimace on either side of his mouth, but around his eyes and all over his face. For the first time I see that a young count can respond as naturally and wholeheartedly as, say, a stable boy.

Something jabs me in the back. Not literally, more in my imagination. There's a rider far in the distance, almost on the morning horizon. Even though it's totally impossible, I think I can make out Sergeant Krauter. That man is driving me crazy.

Dogs rush out to greet us. A powerful voice calls them back. The lieutenant and his second-in-command, a Jager sergeant, are invited into the house. The sergeant comes back out immediately. He orders me to go in there with him. I'm placed between the master of the house and an astonishing straw-gold blond girl at the breakfast table. The splendor! The posh people and the number of dishes! I'm so overcome with embarrassment, I hardly dare help myself to anything. I'm ashamed of how dirty I am and my lack of table manners. I'm ashamed for everything and for me.

The lieutenant explains that three places have been set for visitors, and he simply thought of his servant. Who is partly responsible for the fact that they are now able to eat and in such dignified circumstances. The lieutenant encourages me to help myself, and says that if my hunger is as great as his is, I shouldn't hold back.

The blond girl lays a couple of tidbits on a snow white plate. There's something wrong here. Why for me, of all people? An ordinary officer's valet. She doesn't even turn up her nose, and I'm sure I must stink like a fresh dung heap, or at any rate, like any ordinary stablehand. Can't she smell me? She must. I feel incredibly embarrassed. I have no idea how to approach this fine breakfast among these fine people. In the sixteen and a half years of my life, I have never encountered anything like this before. The lieutenant chews with bulging cheeks. I suppose I'd better start eating. I keep looking over at my lieutenant and the others, and at the girl. I don't need to look at the sergeant. He doesn't know any better than I do. He looks just as sheepish and curious to see how the others are managing. Before long, I see how they use the fine china dishes, and the elegant eating irons. I'm back in heaven. Right at the top. White bread and butter and eggs, and things I'm completely unfamiliar with. But it all tastes heavenly, and I'm glad to be able to make its acquaintance. How good the girl smells. Not like me. Our host and the lieutenant converse largely in French. That's just as well for me, because I don't know any, so I don't have to speak at all.

It's late morning when we take our leave of this hospitable place. I feel so sorry that these nice people, instead of getting our thanks, are having their animals taken away from them. The lieutenant is more sad about it than pleased. I like that about him. Apparently, the young count has a few regular feelings after all.

Two wagons loaded with oats and corn, fifty cows and fifty sheep, and all sorts of other supplies are requisitioned by our forage troop.

The blond girl gives the lieutenant her hand to say good-bye, and then me. Me longer. Was that a bolt of lightning that went through our two hands? I could have died. That's how lovely it felt. I am ashamed and feel happy. The lovely creature didn't despise me, even with my low birth and in my filthy condition. I will never forget that girl's eyes. They looked at me especially fondly. Me, just me.

War is marvelous.

The troop rides off, driving the animals ahead of us, on a way that skirts around the swamp, and back to the regiment.

The colonel promises medals to the lieutenant and the sergeant to reward them for their success.

13.

The days come and go, suddenly it's summer. With hot days, but very cold nights. With hunger and thirst. The requisitioned booty doesn't last us long.

The troops have all come together. Now, thanks be to God, the *Grande Armée* is all there. When the Russian czar sees so many soldiers, he will be terrified and surrender immediately.

Russia is supposed to be somewhere ahead.

So it really exists — I wasn't sure. Incredible, how big the world is. Bigger than the eye can see, the mass of riders and foot soldiers is advancing on the frontier. With musicians and drummers to set the pace. So much noise! The Russians must be fouling themselves in their panic.

I only hope the Russians don't realize how Napoleon's giant army is starving. Apparently, the baggage train has lost touch completely. The forage wagons are creeping along somewhere, several days back. But out of reach. Or perhaps they don't exist anymore, and they're just a story to give the soldiers heart.

The troops are looting.

Every house and every barn near and far is gone over. Whatever's not nailed down is dragged off by the thieves and housebreakers. The soldiers don't care. They belong to the biggest army in the world. Who is going to stop them? Anything they're not given, they take by force. They stick their heads into storehouses, granaries, larders, up chimney flues, they open the cow sheds, pull the carts out of the lean-tos, load them up with supplies, span a pair of stolen oxen in front, and drive the beasts away.

The local people are stripped of everything they own.

According to the rule book, looting is a serious offense. Punishable even by death, in certain circumstances. In the interests of morale. By that token, half the army should be stood against the wall. And of course that's not going to happen. But the generals need a deterrent, before they go on to give the order for the next wave of looting themselves. And so they pick out two or three men who injured themselves in the course of trying to commit suicide. They won't be missed, and perhaps it's even doing them a favor. But first, they have to dig their own graves.

Up ahead is a very big river. Called the Niemen,

according to one person. Someone else says, no, it's the Memel. On the other side is Russia. Finally. The squadron commander rides past my lieutenant and mutters out of the side of his mouth: "Well, here's Russia. Let's hope we don't get lost in that colossus." With a very serious expression, he adds: "Russia's much too big for us. This time, Napoleon's bitten off more than he can chew. We should never have tangled with it."

I would like to ask my lieutenant how big this Russia really is. It may be even bigger than the Holy Land. Even though the whole of the Bible happened there. But you don't ask a lieutenant count questions just because you feel like it. Maybe I'll ask a common soldier sometime, if I think of it.

The riders are unsettled.

"He's supposed to be there."

"Who?"

"Well, who do you think? Napoleon, of course! The greatest commander of all time leading the greatest army of all time."

"One day, we'll be able to boast to our grandchildren that we were with him."

My wellborn lieutenant is trembling with expectation.

"There's a battle ahead of us," he says to himself. "On the other side is the czar with his soldiers. He'll have to turn and fight."

Nothing happens. Neither the czar nor his army are on the other side. I can't see a sausage.

"The Russians have no backbone. They're scared of us. Who in their right mind would take on Napoleon, anyway?"

More and more regiments draw up. With music and drums. The whole plain is black with them. Night falls, and it's an amazing spectacle. As far as I can see, the glow of campfires. Cornets toot commands. Orderlies ride back and forth. The smell of wet wood and charred meat hangs over the site. It's a restless night. Only a few old veterans are able to ignore the excitement. They lie down like old peasants, and sleep in twos and threes.

It doesn't get dark. How can it — with all those fires?

A violent storm breaks. Lightning wriggles over the biggest army in the world. A cloudburst drenches man and beast.

Some say that's a good omen, others say it's bad.

The great battle is hanging over us all.

Gypsy women slink about the camp. They claim to be able to read the future in the palms of the men's hands.

I don't want to know what mine is. The lieutenant has his predicted from the lines on his palm. Then it's my turn. The lieutenant orders me. The beautiful gypsy looks at my dirty hand a long time. Then she looks alternately at me and the lieutenant, and says "Good!" several times.

"What's good?" asks the lieutenant.

"Everything good! You and your brother good," she says in her broken German. She can't mean me when she says "your brother," can she? I'm ashamed. My master is annoyed. I expect he doesn't want to be my brother. Thoughts of the gypsy swirl in my head for a long time. But I don't get any wiser. Nonsense. How is a gypsy woman going to be able to see into the future, anyway? Not even the village preacher can do that, and he's bound to be much nearer to God than any beautiful gypsy woman. And the thing about the brothers gave her away. A count and his servant. It makes me blush with shame.

At daybreak, our sodden regiment reaches the bank of the river that goes by Niemen or Memel. Even though there are several pontoons, the regiments are backed up. And it's still raining on the freezing troops. I wish the sun would come out and burn off the rain clouds.

"Napoleon's already crossed over," someone says.

"He's just now declared war on the Russians."

"Why now?"

"Because that's how it's done. Those are the rules. Napoleon knows what's right."

"So the war's beginning now."

"And it hasn't yet?"

"Those are the rules."

"I wonder what the Russians make of it?"

"Ha, if only we knew. Maybe they don't make anything of it."

"No blood has been shed yet."

"I wonder if the czar will capitulate?"

"If he has any sense, he will."

"Let's hope he does," say some.

"Let's hope he doesn't!" say others. "That would be a pity. After all, we haven't come all this way for nothing. Moscow is said to be an incredibly wealthy city, stuffed with extraordinary treasures. You want to take something home with you, when all's said and done."

"What are we waiting for, then? We just charge across, wipe the Russians out, crush them flat. In an hour, it's all over. Then we move on to Moscow, and fill our boots."

The regiments get into line.

Long boards are rolled up to the river. With their help, the sappers are going to build bridges. Preassembled parts of bridges are trundled along on ox carts. They just need to be slotted together. Let's hope they don't break under the weight of the guns and horses.

A lot of cavalry regiments have already crossed over. "They're forming a bridgehead," the lieutenant tells anyone who wants to hear. Then the cannons creak along after, and the infantry.

"Quick, before the Russians come!"

Midday is sultry. A hot sun comes out and chases away the rain clouds. More showers follow. The uniforms are sticking to our skin. Breathing is difficult. There's too much moisture in the air. In this weather, a man and his horse could both of them molder away. The last scraps of bread rot.

What's keeping the Russians? Napoleon's army churns into Russia and no one opposes us.

No battle.

And no Russians.

The following days remain unpleasantly wet, and the *Grande Armée* is starving.

I manage to get hold of a piece of dry, unmoldy bread. I share it with my lieutenant. Otherwise I think I'd lose him. His stomach growls so loudly, I can hear it several horse-lengths away. He can't beg or steal. He doesn't know how. For his whole life, he's been given everything. And because no one gives him anything now, he has nothing. The supply column is somewhere in the hinterland. It can't keep pace with Napoleon's furious forced marches. From daybreak to nightfall, he is driving us after the Russians.

We bivouac in half-ripe cornfields. Right in the middle of them. That way the riders are at least lying on green stalks and not on bare dirt. The outlying buildings are useless, their roofs have been stripped off, the straw burned or spoiled. The horses eat grass or unripe grain.

Only green stuff, that's all there is. The only change is scraps of wood, birch twigs, or a rotting straw roof. Unless they get hay or oats soon, they'll grind their teeth down on the green fodder. The first kidney ailments are already killing off riding horses and draft animals.

Very warm, and then, scorching-hot days follow. The army is shrouded in clouds of sand. On top of hunger, there is thirst, too. Thirst is much worse. The few wells along the roads are poisoned. In our desperation we drink dirty water from pools and ponds. Trenches are dug in the swampland to collect water. We scoop it up, or just drop our faces into the trenches and drink. The swamp water is brown and lukewarm, and full of wriggly red worms. The more fearful men strain it into their mouths through scraps of canvas.

Every cavalry regiment is issued sickles and scythes. We mow everything down, everything that can be mown and fed to men or horses. We get through a lot. Whatever isn't used up is left to dry or rot. What a waste.

And in spite of that, we are starving. The unripe grain is worthless. It doesn't make flour, and there's no bread without flour. Or anything else. Officers turn a blind eye when their men take off in small groups to steal and plunder. The alternative is to make them starve. The devil take military order.

The men are getting weaker. Every day, the regiments dwindle. Soldiers lie down by the side of the road, or just keel over and die. The thirst! It forces you to drink, no matter if the dirty puddles have corpses or dead horses in them.

It gets hotter still. The dry air trembles over the vast Russian plain. Next to the main roads are dusty corpses. Without lance punctures or saber wounds. Fallen from sheer exhaustion.

Our regiment is riding along in the middle of the army. Everything around is trampled down, cropped bare, burned. Too many men and horses have been this way ahead of us. The regiments at the rear will find nothing at all, beyond the remains of men and animals.

And now, on top of everything, we get the Russians. They sense our weakness. Red-clad Cossacks pick us off from the side.

They are feared like demons. Lying flush to their horses, they gallop up, hack at our feeble troops, and chase away.

My lieutenant is sitting upright in the saddle again. He's forgotten about his thirst for a few moments. Trembling with fear, I press my lance against my hip, but the Cossacks are already off.

The cannons are brought forward. We take aim at the enemy. But they ride like the devil, jagging now here, now there. Hardly anyone is hit. It's like chucking stones at sparrows.

14.

During another Cossack attack, I see him again: Sergeant Krauter. He's fighting grimly, yanking the heavy seven-pound howitzers this way and that with his cannoneers, ramming their muzzles, and firing ball after ball at the Russians.

My lieutenant leaves his platoon and rides up onto a little hill. Maybe he wants a better view of the enemy or just a chance to see what's going on. Or he's looking for a chance to intervene in the scrap, and he's looking around for stray Russians. I stick to his side, because I don't want to leave him, and anyway, that's my place as his servant.

We stand there on top of that hill like a couple of statues, the lieutenant and I. It's not very clever of us.

The sergeant must have seen us. He forgets his

cannons and the enemy, and for a while fixes us with a stare, and then it happens. Krauter shouts something to his gunners. They heave and jerk at the seven-pounder, and point it toward me and the lieutenant.

Has Krauter lost his mind? He's not about to fire at us, is he? Even now, he's filling the cannon's mouth with its death-bringing innards. The sergeant shouts and orders. The howitzer is aimed directly at us.

I think he means it.

Without any respect, I tug at the reins of the lieutenant's horse and yank it down into the nearest hollow. The lieutenant is furious at the incredible disrespect shown him by me, his servant — he's just drawing breath to tear me off a strip — when he hears the ball hit nearby and he sees the earth fly up and then the huge hole in the hillside where we were just standing together a moment ago.

The lieutenant didn't notice what the sergeant was doing. He just says to me: "You did well there! We could have been in trouble." And: "Those Russians have good aim." But I can tell from his eyes that my lieutenant feels something a little more than simple gratitude to me, he just can't talk about it. After all, a count can't get all familiar with his servant and talk a lot of rot.

I'm going to have to be careful around Sergeant Krauter from now on. He is so crazed with hatred, he is capable of anything. Even of using his pretty seven-pound brass howitzer to commit murder.

Two days later, I make a further alarming discovery. No matter how big the army is, there are still truly strange coincidences.

There he is again, the murderous sergeant. But that's not all. He's just overtaking a foot-weary infantry regiment with his howitzer and its team. They are fellow Wurttemburgers. Suddenly, the sergeant stops. An infantryman steps out of the line. The two men know each other, and they have a little chat. I am alarmed. One of them is certainly my mortal enemy, Sergeant Krauter. And, unless my eyes deceive me — and it is quite a distance away — the other is Hanselmann, the cobbler's son from my native village. Now, what have those two got to discuss? Is it a conspiracy against me, or have I started seeing things already?

15.

Blasted war.

My lieutenant's caught one. It doesn't look good at all. It isn't an enemy bullet. Nor a whack with a saber or a jab with a lance. No. The war is rampaging in his innards. Overnight, he's come down with something. Some treacherous disease is messing him up inside. He's slumped in the saddle like an old man on his last legs. His face puffs up and looks greenish yellow, like the yolk of a bad egg. Every so often, he slithers off the back of his horse and drags himself tottering behind a bush. If there is one. What's responsible for his creeping malady is the green stuff we eat and the water from lakes, ponds, creeks, and swamps. He can't take it. The swill rumbles and dins in him so loud that you can hear him feet away, front and back. If the trouble in his belly goes on, he's going to explode.

There are a lot of soldiers in the same boat. Napoleon's *Grand Armée* is not committing any acts of heroism just at the moment. It's too busy stinking up the edges of Russia's main thoroughfares. At least half the troops are squatting down by the side of the road at any given time.

But my lieutenant's even worse off than that. He's so feeble he can't even squat down properly. Is there any way I can help him? If he's so full of poison? I feel sad and apprehensive. I watch fearfully as, slowly but surely, my master is leaving this life. It would really be such a pity for him.

I am baffled. What should I do? Probably, all my lieutenant needs is bread and meat and clean water. It's the filth he has to eat and drink that is destroying him. I don't think there's anything else wrong with him. If he doesn't get anything decent to eat soon, his belly will sour on him, and he'll end up too feeble to drag himself behind a bush to die.

He needs help, fast. Before it's too late. I turn over all sorts of possibilities in my head and can't come up with anything. Stealing? Yes, even stealing. But where can I steal anything from? If only I knew where to find some food. There must be tens of thousands looking for the same for themselves. That's why the tracks of the *Grand Armée* are barren, nothing but desert. The salvation of my lieutenant is perfectly straightforward. I can clearly envision it. Just a decent portion of dinner. A few big chunks of meat, or a doorstop of bread two inches thick, with a quarter of an inch of butter spread on it. Maybe a spoonful of honey to top it off. Served with a billycan of milk, warm from the cow. Followed by a shot of hundred-and-twenty-proof slivovitz to scratch out his belly. All of it good and fresh, and without any mold or red worms. That's all it would take. Feed him like that, and my lieutenant would get better in two shakes. The poor boy. He's in real trouble. I really feel sorry for him. He's so completely helpless, and he stinks to high heaven. It takes all my strength to heave him up into the saddle.

Something needs to happen, and quick. Otherwise I won't have my lieutenant anymore.

There is a surgeon with the regiment. He's under special orders to reattach parts of soldiers or to cut off other parts if he can't fix them up.

I consider: If the surgeon can stitch up and snip off arms and legs, then he probably can take care of the young lieutenant's illness as well. I'm sure he has made a thorough study of people's insides and will know how to quell a mutinous belly.

I ride up to the head of the regiment without too much ceremony, and against all protocol ask the colonel's adjutant for help for my lieutenant. After all, it's a life-or-death situation. The adjutant listens to me and summons the regimental surgeon. Who is an elderly, plodding gentleman, but pretty well preserved and healthy looking. I expect he gets given enough to eat. He comes back with me and looks at the lieutenant for a little while. "A count, is he?" he asks. No other questions. That's all he does. Other than making a face. I start to get a tickling feeling in my head. The man just makes a face and then spouts all sorts of silly nonsense. It is impossible to overlook the fact that the lieutenant is halfway to soldiers' heaven, says the surgeon, quite unmoved, and that he doesn't smell very aristocratic, but really more like a corpse. He, the regimental surgeon, is unable to do much for him, because half the army is suffering in the same way from diarrhea, or a bad case of the runs, as it's also known.

"And so?" I venture to ask him hopefully. "Then the lieutenant doesn't need anything beyond a square meal and clean water. Then he'll be fit as a fiddle again."

"I'm afraid that's right," says the regimental surgeon. "I have nothing to eat myself. No one has anything to eat. There's nothing to be done about that at the moment. Either the count will survive this spell of weakness, or not. Of course, it would be a pity to lose the young man. But then again, we are at war, and war always comes at a price."

And then, to top it all off, he makes me responsible

for his well-being and orders a course of treatment, including, if need be, a ride in a carriage or cart back to Vilnius, so that the lieutenant can be put on a sound diet and nursed back to health — unless, as was all too probable, he happened to have perished in the meantime. "Let's not delude ourselves about that," the regimental surgeon concludes. "The regiment's diarrhea victims are dropping like flies."

And then he gallops off, the regimental quack. Because he's got not just one, but four or five hundred other patients to tend to. When it comes down to it, the whole army's sick.

I have rarely been as angry. I could have done without that wiseacre. You won't catch me going to him to get a leg taken off or reattached. No, sir. He's about as much help as a rat in a granary.

So the surgeon either can't or won't do anything. Except for spout silly nonsense. First, he doesn't need to authorize me to look after my lieutenant. As his servant, I have that authority already. Second, how am I supposed to look after him? He needs food and clean water, which I can't produce out of thin air. And third, where am I supposed to get a coach or cart to take him to Vilnius? Anyway, in the state he's in, he would never make it that far.

The piercing sun comes out from behind the

departing rain clouds. Mercilessly, it boils off the last of the rain to steam, which infests your lungs and makes it even harder to breathe. This steamy air is going to see off my lieutenant. His belly is gurgling and spluttering with damp muck, and in spite of the damp, he's racked with crazy thirst. Then he sweats out the excess water, and I can hear his teeth chatter with cold.

The lieutenant is sagging on his horse.

I'm terribly afraid for him.

We've got to get away from the mess of people, away from the sickly *Grande Armée*. It's all men infected with cholera, anyway, all trying to hold on to life as best they can. No man will do anything for another. And in amongst us all, you can't overlook the bony form of Death.

The next chance I have, I move us off the main army route, and leave the noise and stench behind. We're alone now, the lieutenant and I. There's a dark line on the horizon. Probably a birch forest. That's the only forest there is in these parts. We ride toward it. It will at least give us some shelter. If only, pray to God, there aren't any Cossacks hiding out in it. We're still alone when we get to the edge of the forest. We need to go farther into the trees. The lieutenant and the horses need a chance to get their breath back. I lay the lieutenant on some dry heather. Thank God he's still breathing. He's gurgling and panting in swift alternation. And, unless I've just misheard, he has just whispered some words to his mama, who's no more than a couple of thousand miles away. That's not a good sign.

After our rest, I can hardly can get him back in the saddle. He keeps slipping through my hands. I spend a long time wrestling with him, and thank my lucky stars he's lost so much weight. Finally, I've got him swaying in the saddle. The horses move off, exhausted.

We remain undisturbed. No Cossacks, and no sick, omnivorous *Grand Armée*. Could there be some peaceful, undisturbed stretch of country on the other side of the forest? Where we'll find everything the sick lieutenant needs to get better? We should be out of the forest by nightfall and in our little paradise. If it exists.

I imagine it intensely to myself. I don't think about anything else. There wouldn't have to be roast pigeons. Bread, a piece of bread, would do just as well. I would give the noble Arab in exchange for the life of the lieutenant. And mine, too, of course. Say, for a hunk of bread and a glass of milk each. There's not much time left. I must hurry, while the lieutenant can still breathe and before his belly explodes.

I'm in despair. If only I was as knowledgeable as the wisewoman in our village. She would just have pulled up some roots or plucked a few leaves, and boiled them up into a tea. And got the lieutenant up and about in no time. I'm sorry I'm not a wisewoman.

"Damn, blasted war!" I yell out at the birches and the endless sky. Then I get a grip on myself again. If I curse, I'm sure I won't get anything from the big Whoever behind the birches and the sky. Any child knows that. So, without beating about the bush, I speak a loud prayer for my life and the lieutenant's to be spared. No power, great or small, could ignore such a desperate and passionate plea.

"I'm too young to die, and so is the count!"

Of course, absolutely nothing happens. Nothing like what happened with the youth of Pharnaum in the Bible, for instance. He was even already dead, and then got his life back afterward, and went on to spend many years in health and happiness.

My hopes are withering.

As I sadly and gloomily beg the great expanse beyond birches and sky, I see the snake. It's lying on a slab of stone, completely motionless, a big fat snake. Maybe three feet long. Poisonous? Could be. I only know grass snakes, adders, and measly slow worms. I don't know this Russian variety. Where would I have learned about Russian snakes? I watch it for a while. A beautiful reptile, with a strange pattern on its back. Careful, though. A snake like that might very easily dart up and bite me with its hollow poison-filled teeth. The way the adder does at home.

Then quite suddenly, a strange idea shoots into my head. Roast snake. Of course, roast snake!

I ask the snake to be so good as not to leave its nice slab of warm rock.

It agrees.

After that, everything happens very quickly. I get the lieutenant's saber. The snake is still lying out on the slab of rock. Its tongue flicks out nervously to taste the air. Has it noticed anything? Never mind, it's too late. I catch it directly behind the head. Even so, it jerks up and whiplashes through the air. I'm sure it was dead on the spot. Without a head! I wait a while longer. Better safe than sorry. Then I make a fire of dead birch twigs, wait for it to burn down to hot embers, and drop the snake in it. This style of baking is something I learned to do with potatoes back home. You just had to be careful that the fire didn't get too hot, because then the potatoes would be charred.

I'd never have thought that plain adder would taste so good, without salt or butter. I feed my lieutenant like a child with little peeled morsels of snake meat. He is still capable of swallowing. That's good. Perhaps he senses it's his last chance. The snake does wonders, his breathing comes slower and calmer. That's my impression, anyway.

I'm right! The lieutenant comes back to life. He looks at me in astonishment. I wonder what's going through his mind?

The snake really seems to have been the salvation of

him. I feel much better too. Thank the sky behind the birches! Respectful thanks to the Very Great One!

I am so full of joy, I promise to return the favor through a minister. With my wage. I'll also accompany the next Popish procession I come across, if I ever see another one. Belt and braces! Because, finally, I don't know for certain whether the Almighty inclines more to Lutherans or Papists.

I scan the surroundings for any more snakes. Unfortunately, I can't find any others. All other critters are either too small, or else won't permit themselves to be caught by me.

The one snake hasn't exactly filled us up, but the color really is coming back to the lieutenant's cheeks. Even if he's still like a feeble, cacky baby, life is slowly but surely returning to his veins.

Evening comes. We have to go on and find somewhere that has clean water and a piece of bread. The snake was just a drop in the bucket. If we don't pull ourselves together now, we'll never make it. We'll just perish where we are. And if we're lucky, a Russian peasant may find us in a hundred years' time.

Twilight brings a little freshness to the forest. Still the thirst is burning in our mouths and throats. We're parched.

We can't expect any help from anywhere near here. There's no clean water. Nothing to be seen. Just a few brown, swampy rain holes and froggy ponds. Better nothing than more of that dirty, marshy swill.

The scrubby forest seems endless. More and more birches and juniper thickets, heather clumps and long, sharp grass. It gets a little darker, but not much. That's how summer is here. It doesn't get properly dark. No sooner does the sun go down on the evening side than a red glow appears in the east. In spite of my tormenting thirst, I'm looking for a suitable place to sleep. I need somewhere I can think in peace. It does me no good at all having to push on through the night with the lieutenant. We don't see anything, and quite possibly we're going straight past paradise.

I hear the whinnying of horses. Somewhere ahead of us, but not far ahead. We quickly turn back and ride away a little. Our horses could easily betray us by whinnying back.

Wherever there are horses, there will be people. Cossacks? I hope not. After the initial shock, I become curious. Perhaps it's just other men from the *Grande Armée*. Our side. People like the lieutenant and me. And they may even have something drinkable with them. It's not impossible.

I pack the lieutenant for safekeeping in some half-nibbled heather, tie the horses to a birch, and cautiously set off in the direction where I heard the horses whinnying. I don't hear any more of them, but I soon smell wood smoke. Before long I see flickering light in the dusk. Then I hear a murmur of voices. So the direction was right.

There's a goodly campfire blazing away under the birches. It's rather careless, can be seen and smelled from miles away. Four men are sitting around it. I can't make out the uniforms. Russians' or ours? Why did the men start such a blaze? Because of the wolves? There are said to be as many wolves in Russia as there are voles in our own grain fields at home. I hope the wolves don't get interested in my lieutenant.

Slowly, I move closer to the fire. The men are wearing pretty distressed uniforms. Then shock sends me crumpling to the heather. Those derelict-looking soldiers are wearing the blue of the horse artillery.

Have I lost my mind? Can I no longer trust my eyes? In this endless expanse of forest, miles away from the nearest road, can I really have run up against the man I most wish to the devil? At that campfire sits none other than my archenemy, Sergeant Krauter. He's sitting there, solid and secure, with the firelight dappling him, his voice as loud and harsh as ever it was.

16.

Cossacks I would have found less frightening. They were sort of what I expected. But not Krauter! He's much worse than any Russian. I must not on any account fall into his hands. Whoever aims a cannon against his own side is more dangerous than the worst enemy.

So what are the sergeant and the three transport soldiers doing, so far off the road? Are they on a booty expedition? Or are they trying to get back to Vilnius, as my sick lieutenant was told to do, and sticking to back routes? They certainly don't appear to be in any great hurry.

There's great confusion in my head. I'm shaking with fear and rage and hate. Why is it I keep running into Krauter? It's maddening. But then I come to some more sensible conclusions. I have to get away from here as quickly as I can with my lieutenant. Before Krauter finds us. We'll have to make a big detour around the fire. So we avoid any possibility of contact with them.

It's easier said than done. If only the lieutenant wasn't in such poor shape. He can hardly ride. He sways around on the saddle, and it looks as though he might slip off at any moment. There's no possibility of a canter or a fast trot. He needs something proper to drink first. None of that puddle swill. And then he should be allowed to sleep himself healthy. No, we can't ride off now. We'll have to wait for morning. Besides, we could easily fall into a trap if we ride at night. The Cossacks are bound to be combing the area. In fact, we're in a reasonably good place, so close to that big fire. If there are Cossacks about, they will turn to their visible enemies first. That will give us warning, and the lieutenant and I can run for it. Also, it's certainly better if I don't let the sergeant out of my sight. So we have a little prior warning of what Krauter might undertake next.

If only there weren't this terrible thirst. How can the lieutenant survive it? He must be half dried up already. I hope he doesn't crawl off to a swamp hole in sheer despair, and, in return for a few moments of relief, catch his death of that dreck. I want to get back to him quickly. Also on account of the wolves. On the other hand, I want to get a bit closer to the sergeant and the transport soldiers. They seem to be drinking something with merry abandon. I'm bound that's no puddle water. Either they have found some store of drinkables, or else there's a clean source somewhere in the area.

In the meantime, it's gotten quite dark. The campfire burns brighter.

An odd smell comes winding across the heather and into the birches. A very good smell. It comes to me with the smoke from the fire. Bread? Bread! Only bread smells so good. Freshly baked flatbread or something similar. My head reels. The sergeant and the transport soldiers are baking bread. No doubt about it. The closer I get to the fire, the more indisputable the smell. I almost forget myself. The wonderful smell addles my brain. I'm on the point of walking up to the men and proposing a trade to the sergeant. A cavalry horse in exchange for bread and something proper to drink. That would be a good deal. For both parties. A valuable horse for the sergeant and the prospect of a longer life for the lieutenant and me. I'm sure the lieutenant would have no objection. He wants to get well as soon as he can. His life is worth more even than a purebred horse.

But a flash or spark or some such thing in my brain holds me back from offering this little deal. The sergeant hates me too much. There's no evil action I'd put past him, and no good one I'd expect from him. What if he doesn't give me any bread or water, and just takes the horse anyway? And who knows what else he might want to do? Out here in the wilds, where there's no one to hold him back. He'd have to get rid of me as a potential future witness against him. And who would look after the sickly lieutenant then? No, I'm not going through with it. Krauter's too dangerous.

By now I'm so close to the fire, I can make out the faces. There's no doubt about it. That's the sergeant sitting there. I don't know who the others are, I've never seen them before.

One by one, the four of them are taking big bites out of some chunks of meat and the large flat loaves lying next to them. I'm so hungry and wound up, I start to tremble. I could scream. Not only do the four men have plenty to eat, they're holding mugs, from which they take deep drafts. Next to the sergeant is a little barrel, from which he keeps refilling the mugs. I wonder what it's got in it. Beer? Wine?

A giddy weakness lames me. The fire and the men are swirling this way and that. Which way is up? My belly spasms and growls piteously. My legs won't do what I tell them anymore. Quickly, I drop behind a little birch sapling. Only now do I realize how bad I feel. It's got hold of me as well. Not just the lieutenant. Oh my God!

We need a miracle, a big miracle.

After some time, I come around.

One of the transport soldiers is leaving the bonfire. He moves off into the half-dark. No danger for me, he's going the other way. After a time, he comes back, bringing blankets, in which the four men roll themselves up. So they're going to go to sleep.

Where did the man get the blankets from? They must have been somewhere nearby. My imagination starts to run away with me. I picture a large baggage cart standing by and imagine what things I might find there. Maybe — no, certainly — salvation for my lieutenant and me. I become wide awake. The wildest notions start stacking up in my mind.

Krauter is issuing energetic instructions. Rosters for the night. He and two of the others lie down by the fire. One of them remains sitting. He must be the sentry.

I am very tired, too. But my thirst for whatever is in the barrel and my worry over my lieutenant keep me alert and restless. Is he even still alive? I hope the wolves haven't found him. If they set upon him, he won't stand a chance.

I know what I have to do. Never mind what happens. Somewhere, on the other side of the fire, there must be supplies. I have to find them and help myself to what we need.

I wait a while longer. Krauter and the two soldiers by

the fire are still. They seem to be very tired and are surely fast asleep. The sentry tosses a couple of branches into the fire. The flames get brighter and a little higher.

It's time. I set off on my quest. The baggage cart must be some little way on the other side of the fire. If I haven't made it up. Certainly well hidden and with the horses I heard whinnying earlier next to it. They can't be that far from the fire. On account of the wolves.

The sentry seems pretty relaxed. He can't see me, because he's prodding the fire. That must make him blind to anything else. I make a large detour around the campsite. From time to time, I stop and listen. I need to be careful around the horses, in case I scare them and they start to whinny.

It doesn't take me long to find the cart. And right beside it are the horses, made fast to birches. I count half a dozen of them. Low-set Cossack ponies. Stolen, of course. They turn a little restless, and they whinny happily. Probably they don't much mind who comes out to visit them, so long as it's someone.

The wagon is under a large tarpaulin. I take one more look back at the fire. The sentry is still gazing into the embers. Perhaps he's dropped off too. I can see him wriggling to get comfortable.

Next, things happen very quickly. I climb onto the wagon, get under the canvas, reach here, reach there, touch something round, biggish. Aha! A little barrel. I don't care what's in it. I heave it up onto my shoulders and drag it the long way around the fire and into the forest beyond.

Where's my lieutenant with the horses? I ought to be somewhere near our own campsite. As long as I haven't lost my way. I hope not. Softly, I call out to my horse a couple of times. He answers me with delight. All's well. The lieutenant's still alive. More, he's even capable of speech. The roast snake has done him a power of good. He hasn't been attacked by a wolf, and he hasn't drunk any puddle water, either. His voice is cracked with thirst, but he's feeling better.

He suddenly seems all devoted. He says he was worried about me. And he tells me some of the peculiar things that were going through his mind. He honestly thought I might have run off somewhere without him. Like one of his previous servants.

Stuff and nonsense.

But what luck! The barrel contains wine. It seems it must be quite good wine, at that. At any rate, the lieutenant is gulping it down. I turn the tap off. I want to get some for myself, after all. "It's nectar!" gasps the lieutenant. "I feel completely better. My stomach is cured!"

That's as it may be, but I remain firm. "That's enough now," I decree. "Your Highness doesn't need to celebrate by drinking himself to death."

I'm very happy. My lieutenant really seems to be a whole lot better.

Then I set off back to the campsite again. I have to remember not to sing, I feel so joyful. The sentry has gone to sleep. The fire has died back, because no one has fed it fresh fuel.

The baggage cart is half full of things in sacks and bags. I test a few. I lick my finger, poke around in the bags, and then taste. It's much too dark to see anything. Biscuits and sugar and flour. Miracle after miracle. And oats for the horses. I take some of everything, but not too much, because I still need to be able to carry it, and I don't want its absence noticed right away. I also find a blanket, which I use to carry the things in.

There's activity by the fire. The sergeant has woken up. He's cursing and raging and beating the sentry.

It's time I was gone. Before any of the men goes to check up on their provisions.

The morning sky is already pressing forward after the short night.

Once again, I lug my bounty the long way around the fire. This time, I don't need to look and call. My sense of direction is spot on, and the lieutenant's waiting for me too. He's an intelligent man, and his head is working again. Perfectly rightly, he reasons that after this bold theft we need to disappear as a matter of urgency. Get away, far away. It doesn't bear thinking about, what

Krauter would do to us if he saw us with his goods. I pack the supplies and help the lieutenant onto his horse.

We ride out into a glorious morning. Into a new life. Which way to go? We don't know. Into the sun. East. But clear away from Krauter. The forest looks the same everywhere, sparse and alien-looking. From time to time, we cock an ear behind us in the birches. We make one brief stop, get down off our horses, eat some biscuits, drink some wine. The lieutenant seems to be improving all the time. The way I can really tell how much better he's feeling is the return of his sense of shame. He's noticed himself now that he smells utterly disgusting. And then he laughs so heartily about it that it makes me feel good in my heart. I'm sure that it's not just the return of life and health, but also the cheery, beneficial effect of what's in the little stolen barrel.

"That's enough now, Your Honor!" I say to my almost tipsy lieutenant. "We must try and conserve our wine, and conserve a clear head, what's more. Not least on account of the Cossacks, and Sergeant Krauter."

"Hoo, pardon me!" burps the lieutenant. "None of that Your Honor stuff. I want you to call me Konrad Klara. Because you're almost a brother to me now."

I remember the gypsy girl.

"What does Your Honor want me to call you?"

"Konrad Klara."

"But I can't do that, Your Honor."

"I command it!"

"Very well, Your Honor, Konrad Klara."

"And your name is Georg?"

"No, I'm Adam."

"Adam? Why Adam?"

"It's just my name isn't Georg, it's Adam."

"Just Adam? Nothing else?"

"Just Adam."

"All right. Then I'm going to call you Adam Neve. So that you have a girl's name as well."

"Why a girl's name?"

"Because that's how it has to be! All the boys in our family have always been given their mothers' Christian names after their own."

"I see!"

And then we both laugh. I laugh about Klara, and the lieutenant laughs about Eve.

17.

We don't run into Krauter that week.

We emerge from the forest early one morning. As far as we can see, only pastures and the ruins of wooden huts, their straw roofs cropped by the army horses. Most of the beams were torched on the spot. In the distance is a long, dirty cloud over the endless Russian plain. Dust in commotion. The cloud stretches across the whole horizon, from end to end. As far as the eye can see.

It's the army route, still full of soldiers and all the important and unimportant baggage that the *Grande Armée* lugs along after it.

The lieutenant is well. Better and better! Already he can get on his horse unaided.

"No! I don't want to go to the hospital in Vilnius, I don't need to," he declares. "Why would I, anyway? I'm healthy. Besides, hospitals are bad for your health."

I am skeptical. I mutter to myself, "If the Wellborn Konrad Klara is of the opinion that he's healthy, then I'm sure he's right. And if he says hospitals are bad for your health, then by all means, he doesn't have to go to the hospital. He doesn't have to die now, of course. Now that he's able to mount his horse all by himself."

We ride up to the army road and join the mucky rear guard. Once more our horses have to wade up to their fetlocks in dried dung, and we gulp the thick dust that is stirred up by marching columns, riders, and carriages.

Already by early afternoon, the light seems to be failing. The sun disappears. Even a fresh wind is incapable of dislodging the dust cloud from over the road. It just pushes more smoke and fire reek our way.

"Hey, Adam Neve!" cries the lieutenant. "It stinks abominably. Is the world on fire?"

"Possible! Your Wellborn Konrad Klara."

"Drop the Wellborn, Adam Neve."

"All right, not-Wellborn Konrad Klara."

We hear the rumble of artillery. Somewhere ahead of us. Either side of the road, houses are ablaze, sometimes whole villages. Women and children sit next to the smoking ruins. The lieutenant looks away. He doesn't want to confront such misery.

"Why has God so punished them?" I ask.

"It's not God, it's Napoleon who has punished them. It's part of his great strategy. He pushes hundreds of thousands of soldiers back and forth in divisions and regiments, and leaves scorched earth, dead and wounded, starving women and children. All that is part of his plan."

"I suppose there's no such thing as a decent war."

On the side of the road lie rotting horses and unburied corpses of soldiers. Beside them is an encampment of wounded. Probably on their way back to Vilnius to the hospital. They've built a fire of charred beams, and are just skinning a cat.

On the right is a large birch forest.

We want to stop for a while, and so we take our horses by the bridle and slip in among the trees. Everywhere, there are sick, dying, and dead soldiers. I wish I could have given the sick ones something to eat and a mouthful of wine. But that's impossible — it would be suicide. As soon as we showed anything of our supplies, we would be beaten to death and robbed.

We have to go farther into the forest, then. At last, things get quieter. We don't encounter any Cossacks. They're somewhere else, I'm sure. I don't expect they want to have anything to do with the sick and decrepit. There's no need to go to the trouble of killing them. Only healthy enemies need to be destroyed.

Finally, we're on our own.

I make a little fire of twigs. We don't want to create needless smoke or smell. We knead little cakes and dumplings of flour and wine, and bake them in the embers.

The results are wonderfully crispy. "We really must economize on our wine," I worry. "It's dwindling fast."

Then we return to the army road.

The smell of burning becomes oppressive. There's not a single atom of fresh air in the whirling dirt. The evening haze keeps it off.

All of a sudden, Cossacks come galloping out of the murk, swinging their sabers, and disappear again. The injured soldiers scream in panic for their lives.

Farm carts full of wounded pass us, going back. The wounded have either not been treated at all, or only barely, and their uniforms are soaked with blood.

"What's going on up ahead? Where have you come from?"

"Smolensk. There's been a big battle. The devil of a battle! Three days it raged. We won, we almost won, but too many of the *Grande Armée* are dead or wounded and unable to carry on. Another victory like that will wipe us out."

My lieutenant is becoming restless. No sooner can he crawl like an infant than he wants to be where the action is.

He curses and moans, "Oh, now we've missed the first big battle. Napoleon's gone and won without our help."

I am seized by a great rage. I feel like grabbing Konrad Klara by the shoulders and giving him a good shaking and a talking-to. "Hey, you silly fool!" I want to yell in his face. "You only just managed to give Death the slip, and now you want to chase along after Him!"

But I don't. It would be unpardonable, and I would never be able to set things right again.

Instead, I look sadly at Konrad Klara's glazed eyes. "Don't get all excited, Lieutenant," I comfort him. "There are a lot of battles ahead of us yet, far too many, in fact. So what if we've missed one? Anyway, what would it matter if we missed all of them? Your Wellborn!"

"Don't keep saying Your Wellborn to me."

The evening is bright. The whole country is ablaze. Fires all around. Some are from burning towns and villages, others are where the shattered victors and defeated are warming their bones.

We ride on along the army road to Smolensk, overtaking stragglers, unhorsed cavalrymen, and ragged foot soldiers. We try to overlook the sights of misery by the side of the road, and the wailing and cries for help. A large building is on fire. There are nuns kneeling in front of it, weeping.

"What's the matter with those sisters?"

"Soldiers have raped them."

"Is that war?"

"That's war."

Suddenly, Konrad Klara sobs aloud. How can he still want to fight and be a hero?

116

"Bloody bloody war!" I curse.

Night brings no rest. The smell of fire bites our nostrils and burns from our throats down to the tips of our lungs. We're freezing in our light cavalry uniforms. I'm going to have to find some warm coats. No one would willingly surrender anything like that, so I'm going to have to steal them. The nights are bitter cold again.

In the morning, we move on. The lieutenant is desperate to rejoin his regiment. He doesn't need to squat down by the side of the road anymore. The rebellion in his belly is over, his innards are nicely dried out.

Good.

We're unable to enter Smolensk. The town is turned to ashes. A wooden town burns easily. Only the remnants of copper roofs lie scrolled up next to the ruins. We ride through the outskirts of Smolensk, heading toward Moscow now. Barefoot infantrymen are sitting by the roadside. Fellow Wurttemburgers, to go by the uniforms. The lieutenant stops and questions a lieutenant of these ragged troops. He doesn't exactly look like a hero, and he doesn't know much, either, but he is able to tell us that it's mid-August, give or take a day or two, and that Napoleon is rushing toward Moscow like a madman to catch up with the Russian army. He needs to defeat it and force the czar to sue for peace. With a sigh, the other lieutenant adds: "Napoleon has to make peace, and fast! Otherwise we're all done for."

117

The passage of the *Grand Armée* is clearly marked. Impossible to mistake, and ghastly. Thank God the road dust obscures a lot of the misery from sight. I need to be careful I don't lose my lieutenant in the dirt and smoke. He's in a tearing rush. Going faster and faster. What is it that makes him hurry like a madman — and to his possible doom, what's more? He'd be better off to try and avoid the fight and be pleased he's been spared, so far.

Two days later, we catch up with the remains of the army. We even find our own regiment, after a little searching. It's a pretty sorry sight, consisting of a small group of men and a handful of horses. Ripped and ragged like a bunch of highwaymen. "Fought too bravely," moans the platoon commander. "And all for nothing!" He rides up close to the lieutenant, and whispers in his ear: "You know, we should be fighting against Napoleon, and not against the Russians." My lieutenant looks about him in alarm. Hopefully, no one else heard. Apparently, Napoleon has spies everywhere.

It's not much farther to Moscow now.

There, the Russians will once again have to give battle, say the regimental officers. Definitely! They can't allow their capital city to fall into Napoleon's hands. It's sacred to them.

"The campaign will be decided at the gates of Moscow. We will be victorious, and be richly rewarded for the sacrifices and privations we've had to endure," the officers and men all hope. "Moscow is immeasurably rich, and we will take some of its treasures back home with us."

It turns into a pleasant evening. Our platoon is bivouacked next to the smoking beams of a farmhouse. I dig up our treasures. We bake the rest of our flour and share the warm flatbread and the rest of our biscuits with nine reasonably fit comrades. We wash them down with wine, of which there's one mugful per man. And suddenly, its magical powers creep into us and, for one fleeting moment, conjure up visions of a happy and livable future.

Then I am torn out of my happy reverie with a jolt. A cold shiver runs down my spine. Sergeant Krauter is standing behind my lieutenant, staring as if hypnotized at the little wine barrel. I think I must be seeing things. I wipe my sleeve across my eyes and scatter the campfire smoke. No, there's no sergeant. I must have been deceived. But it takes a while for the shock to melt away. To the devil with him, I say to myself. I'm not about to have waking nightmares about that rogue. I drink down the last of my wine and wash away the Krauter ghost.

18.

My lieutenant is surplus to requirements. He has no more men left to command. His platoon consists of two horses, himself, and me. It doesn't take much imagination to appreciate that the only reason we're still alive is because the lieutenant's belly gripes ensured that we missed the battle at Smolensk.

The regimental commander comes by in person to take a look at the lieutenant. The two of them are well acquainted. In fact, it turns out one of them is the uncle, and the other is the nephew. The wellborn colonel is reasonably pleased with his nephew's state of health. Even so, he pulls a face, and scolds him in French and German, of which I only understand the German. "Thunder and lightning!" he snorts. Had his nephew taken leave of his senses when he ignored the order to report to the hospital in Vilnius and get himself cured? And had he instead taken off after the army, to meet his death with it? Then he wrinkles up his nose, sniffs at his nephew, and barks in disgust: "Thunder and lightning! It's high time my nephew changed back into being a respectably scented lieutenant, got rid of his filthy gear, and cleaned himself up."

In less elegant language, I am instructed to put the lieutenant and his tunic into militarily acceptable shape. After all, it is the foremost duty of an officer's servant not to let his master run around in such foul condition.

We go looking for a suitable lake. The first is too close to the highway. Too many filthy foot soldiers and whole cavalry regiments, including horses, have already availed themselves of it. The water looks like it, and it stinks horribly. This lake wouldn't exactly get us clean, so we look farther afield. And because the war is just now in a phase of relative calm, the colonel has left us a whole day to that end. So we have plenty of time to do our laundry, and we don't need to stop at the first puddle we see.

The second and third lakes don't impress us, either. In the second there are bodies of men and horses floating about, looking none too healthy. The third smells bad, and its shores are muddy. Whereas what I'm looking for is a clean spot for my laundry, with fine sand. After all, I need something to scour the clothes with. The fourth lake is a long way from the highway, and accordingly clean, with a sandy shore. And it has the great advantage of being deserted. Just a dozen or so cranes promenading along the shore.

Just to be safe, we observe the lake and surroundings from a distance. No Cossacks or Bashkirs or other people. No suspicious movements in the adjoining forest, either. So we have the lake to ourselves, and I can wash uniforms in peace.

Somewhere in the distance there's a whump of artillery. I wonder if another battle is in progress? Never mind. It's so far away that it doesn't concern us, and we don't need to think about it. But the faraway noise rapidly comes nearer. It seems to be from due east. Maybe not too far from Moscow. With all this banging, it has to be quite a big show. Probably it's another battle after all. Definitely. All those gunpowder explosions and masses of rifle shots. We can even hear the signal trumpets when the wind is from that quarter, and the drumbeats calling on regiments to fire.

The lieutenant wants me to make haste. Because of the battle in the distance. He doesn't want to miss out on another important battle. Not again.

"First we have to wash. Ourselves and our clothes. Those are orders from His Excellency the colonel in person."

"But let's be quick about it."

Of course I have to wash both uniforms. A lieutenant isn't a washerwoman. That's what he has his servant for, which is me. Only now do I see how much dirt has found room on and in his uniform. Even the very fine lake sand can't seem to dislodge it. It's by no means an easy task. I'd much rather muck out ten stables than have to scrub a pair of white cavalry lieutenant's pants. Without benefit of soap or cauldron or any of what you would normally require for a sound wash. Well, the dirt won't go. Soak, therefore. I dunk the uniform in the shallow water, and place a large stone on top of it. The dirt will surely have to dissolve and leave the fabric. You'd think. It doesn't, though. More sand treatment. But only up to a point. Because it looks as though the material is being rubbed away, and only the dirt survives intact. Such filthy, stained trousers really are a disgrace.

The distant rumbling is getting louder all the time, crashing and banging like some heavy thunderstorm. There seems to be something going on. And we, Lieutenant Count Lammersdorf and I, his servant, are once more not at the scene of the action.

Thank God! Although of course I don't say so.

"That must be Moscow over there," reflects the lieutenant.

"You could be right about that."

The summer is pretty done up. In Russia it's not like

it is at home, anyway. The sun pushes itself through the last few days of it. Unenthusiastically, or even under protest. It's certainly not prepared to shed any warmth. Unless it makes a bit of an effort, it's not going to get our uniforms dry. I drape our pants across a bush in the sunshine. From time to time, a light, warmish wind blows by.

What applies to our trousers applies to ourselves, too. We, too, need to lie and soak for a long time. The water is still tolerably warm. It's stored up some of the warmth of July and August. It's warmer in the water than it is outside, in the keen east wind. The skin takes a while to soften and start to resemble skin again. Konrad Klara can swim. He tells me it's something he learned to do in the noble fishponds at home. I too, am able to keep my head above water, so we have a high old time splashing and jumping about like little children. Konrad Klara quite forgets himself and forgets the battle too. He whoops and splutters, and I forget about the battle myself. There's a small island in the middle of the lake. Of course, we decide we have to swim to it. It turns out to be farther away than we thought. We come ashore panting, and then look back to the bank.

"It's a damned long way! Doesn't it look small."

"It was fun, though, even if it was tiring."

"Yes, it was fun all right! I've never swum this far in my life."

"Hold on a minute. Are you sure you're looking at the right bit of the bank?"

"Yes, quite sure."

"I don't believe you! Then our horses ought to be standing tethered to those trees. But they're not there."

With bad premonitions, we strike out for the bank.

The horses are gone.

"Did you tie them up somewhere else?"

"No! I'm sure it was here. Look, you can still see the hoofprints in the sand."

"And the uniforms that you put out to dry on the juniper bush?"

"Gone as well!"

"Everything gone!"

"Our money too!"

Never in all my life have I had so much money as now. Only yesterday the paymaster caught up with us and gave us our back pay for six months. I got ten Albert thalers. At home, I could have bought an orchard or a meadow with that, and a couple of sheep, and, if prices were low, then a couple of cows as well. The lieutenant is even worse off than I am. He had a fortune with him. Over a thousand gulden. That's a heck of a lot!

We run around the shore like two madmen.

Everything gone. Everything.

We have nothing at all. We're standing there buck naked.

"Someone must have robbed us!"

"Cossacks or Bashkirs?"

"I don't think so. The Cossacks would have waited for us and drowned us in the lake. A sneaky theft like that just isn't their way of doing things."

"But who was it, then?"

"Maybe some local farmers, or bandits."

"Bloody war, having to run around stark naked!"

We hurriedly hide ourselves in some bushes, and watch the edge of the forest. In case Cossacks are around. Or Bashkirs, for that matter.

The plain is deserted. Nothing to be seen. But someone must have been there and picked up our horses and the uniforms with them.

And I took so much trouble with the laundry. Maybe the thieves would have left the lieutenant's trousers if they'd still been all filthy.

I swear horribly.

The many cannons are still booming away in the direction in which apparently Moscow lies.

"My beautiful Arab horses," whimpers Konrad Klara.

"How will we get back to the regiment?"

"It was half a day's ride. Without horses, without clothes, barefoot. Impossible! We'll never get back to the regiment."

I could weep.

Konrad Klara does.

A weeping lieutenant. I wonder what the king of Wurttemburg would say to that? Or even Napoleon himself?

19.

We wait till it's almost dark. The great plain is deserted. Most likely the robbers took their departure through the forest and rode off beyond. Hopefully. Or else they're still in the forest. Hopefully not. We couldn't put up any sort of resistance. Just with our bare hands. Our weapons are gone too.

"No one around. No Cossacks. No Bashkirs."

We have to make the most of the gathering darkness. So that we remain unseen by Cossacks, Bashkirs, or any other people, for that matter. Naked as we are, we have every cause to feel shame. Even though we're not to blame.

Barefoot and hungry, we set off on our way. It's gotten damnably cold. Now the sun's gone, there's an icy wind out of the east.

"Straight from Siberia," says Konrad Klara. "I expect it's already blowing over ice fields there."

"Siberia!" I exclaim. "Do you mean there's yet another country beyond Russia?"

"Bound to be," trembles Konrad. "And others beyond that, too."

"All the things you know!" I envy Konrad Klara.

Konrad Klara is shaking with cold. In spite of the falling darkness, I can see that he's all covered with goose pimples. His teeth are rattling and chattering.

I'm not too good myself. I could use a thick fur coat, like the estate manager's wife had in Schonbronn. And warm socks and shoes and all those other things that keep a body warm. But we have nothing. Nothing whatever. Not even a handkerchief between us. Konrad Klara needs a lesson from me in how to blow your nose without one of those little kerchiefs. It's an important lesson, because our noses are starting to dribble in the cold. The stable boys at home always snot themselves like that, and the common soldiers do the same. They all of them blow their noses with their fingers. Has he never seen it done before, Konrad Klara?

"Adam Neve," he says. "I'm really cold."

"I am, too. Russia is a cold country. Even though summer can hardly be over. We'll have to run to warm up."

But Konrad Klara can't keep it up for very long. He

gets slower and slower, and starts to lag behind. His recent illness is still in his bones. His breath comes short and whistling.

I don't like it. A farmhand from Morbach had that whistling in his lung once. He was very quickly suffocated by it. Or at any rate, he died from it. Konrad Klara's panting and wheezing sounds a lot like that.

"I don't want my lieutenant to die!" I quietly beg the Great One behind the birches and the infinite sky above. Maybe it helps. I have fared well with it in the past.

Did we come from here or from there? No idea. This Russia looks the same all over. Best thing is to head for the barking cannon. Stands to reason. Where there's a battle, there'll also be an army.

If only it weren't so cold. We alternate between running and walking. The chill creeps up out of the ground like cold breath.

In Russia, a man isn't made for naked living.

There's no point. Konrad Klara can't go any farther. My blood seems to be freezing too. We've gone as far as we can. We have to warm ourselves up now, in a hurry.

But how, without a fire?

There's a little wood ahead of us.

"We'll camp in there."

"I'm freezing," trembles Konrad Klara.

"You won't freeze that quickly, Your Wellborn."

"Don't call me that always," he says crossly.

The early evening has no stars. It doesn't need any. The battle is still raging in the distance and lights up the whole eastern half of the sky. The armies are making their own light.

"Damned war," I curse. Konrad Klara doesn't contradict me. Instead, coughing hoarsely, he agrees, "Damned war," and he shakes so hard his skin wrinkles.

I look around in the little wood. Not a soul in there. It's safe to spend the night. I break off soft branches, pile old leaves into a heap on top of them, pull moss off the ground and layer it over the leaves. A few more branches on top to keep the whole thing in place. And then we slip under the little hill.

Konrad Klara continues to chatter a while longer. But before long he calms himself. His breathing comes regularly. We get warm in our little earth tent. We'll survive the night.

The morning is quiet. No more sounds of the battle for Moscow. It seems to be over. The sun climbs out of a thick mist. It lights us with feeble autumn rays. The smoke from yesterday's battle has robbed it of most of its strength. Even so, it has a little warmth left over for Konrad Klara and me. Hunger and thirst soon get us going.

No one to be seen. All morning not a soul. Once, a couple of red-clad Cossacks gallop past a long way off.

Just in case, we press ourselves down to the ground. We're not spotted. Who knows what Cossacks would do to a couple of naked enemies?

The battle really does seem to be over. The thunder from the cannons has completely stopped.

Hunger scratches at our stomachs. I'm ready to eat grass. The thirst is still worse. But we don't drink anything. We've already experienced the consequences of doing that.

Late in the afternoon, we come to a village. I want to try to steal a couple of pairs of pants, and maybe something to eat and drink as well. Konrad Klara is opposed to stealing, but we both need something to wear. The door of the first house is bolted. The second likewise, it's not possible to open any of the doors. I look for a tool with which to try and force one open. Just in time, I spot the group of men armed with clubs. They're waiting for me in the next house. I hurriedly walk away. After a few yards, I start running.

How are we going to get hold of some trousers? If only we had money or something to offer in exchange!

"Oh, Adam Neve," Konrad Klara says. "Don't take it so hard. In the Bible, Adam and Eve were both naked as well. We shall just have to get used to it." After a while, he adds: "If only it were a bit warmer." And he coughs some more.

Konrad Klara won't be able to stand much more of this naked living. He cools down so quickly. I keep thinking of the wheezing breath of the stable boy from Morbach.

Toward evening, we reach the edge of the great plain. A fine peaceful sunset lies over the country. At last we've reached our objective. We've managed to rendezvous with the army again. In the distance in front of us, there are soldiers covering a hill. They're lying all over the slope, horses, too. Hundreds, thousands? Are they resting from the battle, or are they waiting for the next one to begin?

Cautiously, we approach them. We feel ashamed on account of our nakedness. But the men don't pay us any attention. The whole area smells terrible.

What regiments do they belong to? Look at the uniforms!

"Ours?" Konrad Klara and I wonder, at exactly the same moment.

But we don't see any Wurttemburgers. Only French, Westphalians, Prussians, and . . .

"Look, there, Adam Neve. Those are Russians, aren't they?"

"Russians?"

"Beyond a doubt! Russian foot soldiers."

What are Russians doing in the midst of Napoleon's army?

"They're all dead!" screams Konrad Klara.

And then I notice bloodied bodies, severed arms, heads blown off by cannonballs. Beside them, a ditch. Lots of arms and legs and whole bodies lying in it. Probably a doctor was working on them until a few moments ago. I feel chilled to the bone, and then a hot sweat comes over me. I can hardly speak.

"Oh, Konrad Klara," I manage to say. "We're on the site of yesterday's battle."

Konrad Klara is shaking from top to toe.

"So many," he groans.

He suddenly leans against me. He presses his face against my bare chest, and stands there a while, without moving. Then he leaps away.

Is he ashamed?

"Damned war!" shouts the young Lieutenant Count Lammersdorf.

I go up to him and drag him away from the corpses. The battlefield is too gruesome. Up on the hill, something is moving. Wolves are nosing around.

How many young men have been slaughtered here? Have all these soldiers let themselves be shot for the sake of Napoleon? Now they're lying peaceably among the enemy, next to them and on top of them. Apparently, not everyone is dead. There's moaning and wailing and screaming coming from a bloodied bundle. We can do nothing. What could we do? Away from this place. These scenes mustn't dig too deeply into our memories. Otherwise they will remain with us as long as we live.

Amazing. In spite of the thousands of dead bodies all around me, I have a dreadful idea. There are so many trousers lying here, some bloody, some clean. Depending on whether the soldiers were shot in their upper or lower halves. All I need to do is take them away from a dead man. Simple.

Then I suddenly feel my belly heave. I sit down on an empty spot on the battlefield and vomit up half my stomach.

For his part, Konrad Klara can hardly walk, but he helps get me back on my feet.

Bare and naked we stumble about among the mutilated heroes.

I narrow my eyes to the merest slit. So that I don't see everything. I'm only out for suitable trousers. Most of them are no use at all. They are slashed, holed, or sodden with blood. But here's a pair that might do for my lieutenant. Their wearer has been shot in the chest. The trousers didn't take any damage. Now's not the time to hang around. Yes or no. Stay naked or rob the dead. I drop to my knees in front of the dead soldier, and pull at his trousers. I'm in a hurry. I want it to be over. Fortunately, it's pretty dark. That way I can't see the dead man's face. The trousers are fashionably tight. I can't get them over the shoes. So shoes off, too. They are good shoes. They might fit me. I try them on. They're still warm. Why warm? The soldier twitches. He's alive.

My head spins and everything goes black. I throw the shoes down and crawl away.

20.

All around, it's once again a chilly night. I can't take much more. I'm freezing to death. Hunger. And thirst. Life is already making a large detour around me. And Konrad Klara is incapable of anything except shaking. He's stopped speaking and is just staring into space. I wonder what's to see there? The end? But before my end, I'd rather crawl up to a filthy hole and drink. Enough of this torture.

The dead soldiers on the hill and the severed arms and legs disappear in the darkness. But there are stirrings of life out there. Creeping shadows. Those are wolves. I fear for Konrad Klara. I sit right close to him and warm him a little. And he me. It makes barely any difference. Neither of us has any warmth to share, we're both half frozen. And the wolves are coming nearer. I see glittering eyes, quite close now.

Soon it will all be over. I cling on to Konrad Klara.

A torch shines in my face.

"Here's another survivor." I hear someone shouting above me. "And another one."

"Isn't it an outrage," says someone else. "They stole the uniforms off their backs. They're half frozen to death."

I am wrapped in a coat and carried off. Slowly, I warm up again. Someone has set me down beside a large fire. Konrad Klara is lying next to me.

Suddenly, I want to live again.

Later on, we are brought hot broth from a large cauldron. Or maybe it's just herb tea. I don't care. Anything would taste wonderful to me. But the drink has a miraculous effect. My thirst is gone, my hunger's gone. Konrad Klara is lying stretched out in front of the fire. I think he's even smiling.

21.

Two days later, we're both up and about, the lieutenant and me, his servant. A sergeant has been instructed by the colonel to get us both some uniforms. Never mind which. Soldiers can't run around naked under someone else's borrowed overcoat, after all. We've both been found uniforms that befit our rank. Konrad Klara has become a Portuguese lieutenant, while I am now a French private. I suppose there didn't happen to be any Wurttemburg tunics available. It wouldn't matter so much with the pants. Pants are pants. But the caps and helmets and insignia, the sashes across the breast and all the detail of a uniform, all that makes a difference. Neither uniform is exactly new. Soiled and grubby, to be precise. My French tunic has a scorch mark on the left shoulder, and I can only bring myself to slip into the trousers if I look the other way, or better, if it's completely dark. I would never entrust my legs and behind to such filthy quarters under any other circumstances. Still, the nasty things are better than nothing at all, because it's true that naked soldiers freeze faster than their uniformed fellows. I have the suspicion that our new gear was taken off dead men. On the back of the Portuguese tunic my lieutenant wears there's a dark round bullet hole. The hole is fringed with marks of gunpowder scorch and dried blood. The Portuguese lieutenant must have been shot from behind.

Of our once proud regiment of mounted Jagers, all that remains is a feeble company of more dead than alive cavalrymen and a few spindly nags.

Apparently, there's also a shortage of servants in the army. An elderly major insists he wants me in his service.

No, please, not for all the tea in China! I'm terrified. Then I would have to trade in my wellborn lieutenant. Unfortunately, there's nothing I can do about it. Turn down the major? That would be insubordination, and I'd be shot for it. Now it all comes down to what Konrad Klara says.

"I'm not going to surrender my servant, the cavalryman Georg Bayh," says Lieutenant Count Lammersdorf. "Not under any circumstances!" It would take an express command, he tells the major, and even then he might for the first time in his life have the pleasure of disobeying.

I'm so happy. I could fling my arms around the

lieutenant's neck. Of course, I do no such thing, because between an officer and his servant, that's out of the question. The world would end first.

The major is sore. He says he's a count himself, and furthermore a long-serving senior officer decorated with the Croix d'Honneur, whose own servant had his head split open by a Cossack the day before yesterday at the battle of Borodino, leaving him short, and there wasn't a single respectable servant in the whole regiment, except for the aforementioned cavalryman Bayh, who, in the natural order of things, should be with the senior officer, and not with some little baby officer who was still wet behind the ears.

There is a scene between the major and the lieutenant. Finally, the youngest lieutenant in the Wurttemburg army gets to have his way. The colonel is his uncle, after all, and moreover, a sensible man. He decides the argument by not deciding it. No one gets the servant. Which again isn't quite true, because everything is left more or less as it was. The colonel, after a brief word with the major general, promotes me to corporal. On account of particular bravery on several occasions, and with immediate effect. As a corporal, I can't be anyone's servant, neither a lieutenant's, nor a long-serving major's.

Clever. Konrad Klara and I continue to ride together in the regiment, not far behind the colonel. We're pleased;

the major is annoyed. Another one we both need to keep an eye on.

The war goes on.

Most of the regiment's horses are lying on the side of the road somewhere, on a battlefield, or they've run off or been stolen, or they've wound up roasted over a campfire and eaten. I could weep when I remember the proud condition of the regiment as we moved out of Ludwigsburg, barely six months ago. And now! All gone.

Of course, the regiment has managed to pick up a few new horses. But they're just puny little things. I'm sitting on one, a little steppe pony. It's unkempt, short-legged, and shaggy. Probably used to be a Cossack or Bashkir mount before. It's not much to look at, and a rider with long legs would have to keep pace with his feet, or else brake with them. But I'm still lucky in my horse. He's so small that no one wants him to begin with. He doesn't exactly look cut out for a cavalry regiment. Something so puny. But he's a plucky little devil. If I show him the whip, he turns into a giant eagle and skims over the ground. He's got a good heart too. After the first day together, we're agreed, the little steppe pony and I: We belong together.

Konrad Klara has been given a bigger horse, but he has much more trouble with it. Maybe it's sensed that he doesn't like it. Of course, it's nothing like the noble

Arab that he is used to riding. I'm sure the animal can sense his aversion.

We are caught out by the Russians. They are firing down at us from up on a hill. Our regiment has walked into an ambush, as onto a plate. The horsemen scatter. They melt away before the cunning bombardment. The colonel doesn't like that at all. He observes the situation for a while. Then he gets into a rage, and when he gets into a rage, he's a man transformed. He turns his horse around and makes for the cannon. His decrepit regiment follows him. Eighty rickety untrained steppe ponies, with famished, sickly riders clinging to their backs. At their head, the colonel gallops straight at the enemy cannon. By the time the heavy cylinders can be pointed at the attackers, it's too late, and they've been cut to ribbons. It's the first time I've used my saber in anger. Each time I bring it down, I look the other way. So I don't have to see any of the faces. A face might easily stick itself in my brain, and maybe I'd never get rid of it. Then I'd have to think of it, and ask myself why I had to chop at that particular human being.

But my bad conscience fades quickly. After a few blows, I feel used to smiting and killing. My own head has become strangely unfamiliar. On the inside it's completely empty and feels nothing, while under the helmet, there's a pounding in my temples like heavy artillery. I haven't touched a drop, and yet I am completely sozzled.

My lieutenant has very sad eyes. He's swishing and slicing like a maniac. He rides right up to me, and bellows: "Damned war!"

Then I'm back to normal again, and I'm glad the lieutenant exists. But most of all, I'm glad Konrad Klara takes no pleasure in killing.

"Your Wellborn Konrad Klara," I call back. "Look after yourself, and guard your life! You'll have need of it in the future."

He laughs, and fends off the saber thrust of a Russian like some old warhorse.

The regiment's casualties are just one horse and three men. But even that's more than war is worth.

Some French marshal watches our attack and is so impressed, he pulls the golden Legion of Honor off his chest that he got from Napoleon in person, to give it to the colonel. But the colonel looks at the marshal as contemptuously as if he were just one of many day laborers on his estate, gives his horse the spurs, and rides off. The marshal is bewildered. Then his eyes light on me, and because he takes me for a Frenchman in the uniform, he rides up to me. Is he going to give me his medal? That's not allowed in any case. A common soldier isn't allowed to receive such a thing. The marshal doesn't catch me, anyway, because, like the lieutenant, I present my back and bottom to him and hare off after the colonel.

22.

On the orders of some Napoleonic marshal or other, our regiment rides from morning till night. Like the rest of the *Grande Armée*, inasmuch as they're mounted. Always in pursuit of victory and looking for a decisive engagement. But victory isn't what it was, and the decisive battle doesn't come.

"There's Moscow up ahead!" the colonel says to his officers.

Where? Around the edge of the forest? No. Behind the next hill? Not that, either. The colonel just wants to encourage his regiment.

The troops need to be pumped up for battles and rage against their enemy. Otherwise they won't fight properly. And they need to know where they're going. Moscow is useful as a destination. The objective of this war. It beckons to us with its magnificence and its huge treasures. Every last man in the *Grande Armée* knows that.

But perhaps Moscow doesn't exist, and Napoleon has simply made it up to keep his men in line.

But then the regiment canters out of a forest, and suddenly there's Moscow at our feet.

Extraordinary. All the things there are in the world! An enormous city stretches from one side of the horizon to the other: the longed-for, oft-doubted, rich and sacred capital city of Russia. The one on whose account the *Grande Armée* has marched and ridden so many miles.

My heart starts to beat faster.

The dying rays of the sun are falling on the beautiful city. As far as I can see, all the streets are in dead straight lines, and it's just one house after another. Most of the houses are wood, many of them have straw roofs. In amongst them there are some lofty stone buildings, and numerous golden church towers, sparkling onion domes with gold orthodox crosses. The sea of roofs shimmers peacefully under heaven's light in the evening sun. Much too peacefully.

There's no trace of the czar and his armies.

The colonel is annoyed.

"When are we going to have our battle?" he keeps asking. "Surely the czar will have to defend his capital city! That's what the form is. Are the Russians really so unfamiliar with the rules of war?"

The major, riding at his side, adds: "Every Russian is duty bound to give up his last drop of blood for such a city."

But the Russians don't give battle and don't shed a single drop of blood for their Moscow. And the czar stays out of sight. He doesn't do what Napoleon wants him to do. Apparently, he has a different view. At any rate, he won't be told what to do.

French Guards move past us. Brazenly, they ride straight for Moscow. They are rested and well fed and presentable looking. Their uniforms have yet to be dirtied by any battle. Their horses step out lightly. As if it were the barracks yard or some parade in Paris. Napoleon's lifeguards are a military feast for the eyes. In their midst is a squat little man in a gray uniform.

"Is that Napoleon?"

"Bound to be! Who else could it be?"

Is he really so ordinary? If he weren't surrounded by those proud lifeguards, you wouldn't give him a second look.

A soldier in the next regiment shouts out: "Huzzah!" Farther off, someone else calls: *"Vive l'Empereur!"*

In spite of myself, I feel gooseflesh going up and down my spine.

So that's him, the renowned French emperor. The one before whom all Europe trembles.

"He will meet the czar at the city gates," predicts the

major. "The czar will capitulate, and the city elders will present the keys of the city to Napoleon. On a golden cushion, of course. That's the way these things are done. And then there will be peace, immediately thereafter."

My lieutenant is moved.

I always knew it: Konrad Klara doesn't belong in any war. Certainly not in this one. He is much too soft-hearted.

"Your Wellborn Konrad Klara," I say to him, "now we can go home soon. In another couple of hours, the war will be at an end."

"Drop that Wellborn, will you!" Konrad Klara scolds me.

I feel happy. As never before in my life.

"There'll be a triumphal procession," I say, thinking aloud. "When we move into Stuttgart as victors, and our Very Highest Selfsame Majesty has us parade in front of his castle."

I lose the thread of my thoughts. I wonder if the king is still so fat? Why wouldn't he be? He never has to suffer hunger. And I'm sure he's unacquainted with the runs. Not to mention pond water full of wriggling red worms.

In spite of my joy at the end to the war, I still manage to feel a little bit sad. It occurs to me that my lieutenant is bound for one place, and I am bound for somewhere else. The moment the war is over. Almost a shame.

Order from some French marshal: The Wurttemburg regiment is not to advance into Moscow. We are to remain on the heights at the edge of the broad-leaved wood in readiness.

A passing general says we have to shield the French emperor from possible surprise attacks. Or are we only to be admitted to Moscow once the city has been plucked bare? Perhaps by Napoleon and his Guards in person?

We bivouac on the heights. Apparently, it was Marshal Ney in person who chose us for this strategically important role. All around, sentries are set up. Who can say what cunning plans the Russians might have, in spite of the imminent peace?

So the regiment guards the road that leads down into the city. The cavalrymen set up camp and light fires, warm themselves, and gaze down at the city.

Nothing happens.

What about peace? We can hear and see nothing. The bells should be ringing, the soldiers cheering, cannons banging out the triumph. Trumpets should be blowing the command to the victory parade!

But nothing. Deathly silence.

Gradually, doubts start to come. The uncertainty feeds the oddest and craziest rumors. Will the czar make peace, once the city is in Napoleon's hands? Or is the war not yet over? Maybe there are complications in the peace negotiations; Napoleon is said to be insatiable. A few old skeptics don't believe this is victory. Victory doesn't look like this, they complain. And Russia can't be conquered, in any case. The country is much too big. Even for Napoleon. The little upstart has bitten off more than he can chew.

The city turns gray. With the last of the sun's rays, the colors disappear. The gold on the towers and minarets pales and then completely disappears in the dusk.

Suddenly, the evening sky brightens up again, this time from the direction of the city. A different light is boiling up from there. Fire is flickering up through roofs, smoke billows and swells into clouds. The dying light of day hurriedly turns into firelight. The wooden houses and their straw roofs are well alight. Each one torches its neighbors. Or is some devil setting fires? The whole of Moscow is suddenly ablaze, even the part of it that is on the opposite side of the river, which is called the Moskva.

I am so amazed, I forget to breathe, and gulp in the air I need. What a terrible, magnificent sight! Has any man ever seen such a thing? "Nero," says Konrad Klara. But I don't know any Nero.

So much fire all at once! As if the sun had fallen. Fear and horror. What a shame for the beautiful city! God be merciful to her. All her riches are burning.

The fire oppresses my soul. I'm sure the others are feeling no different. They must guess, if they don't know, that peace looks different. Not like this, for sure.

The colonel gets on his horse. He peers intently into the spreading sea of flames. Horse and rider are each tense. Then they gallop off. The major wants to ride after him, but the colonel waves him away.

Bad premonitions wrap themselves like iron bands around my chest. Konrad Klara, too, is looking distressed by the sight of the world on fire. Sad and anxious, he says: "Victory and peace are going up in flames down there."

The colonel doesn't return till midnight. He looks tired and exhausted, and he stinks of smoke and soot. Without any elaborate explanations, he assembles a detachment of men. The *troupe*, as the French call it, is to bring up supplies, under the command of a sergeant.

"Hurry!" orders the colonel. "There's not much time. Some of the burned and burning buildings have stores in their cellars," he says. "These are all being plundered now. We must not be the last."

The sergeant has to set off with his men right away.

"And get hold of some schnapps!" the colonel calls out after the detachment. "So that we can drown our sorrows. Our future is not something to be contemplated in a sober state."

Then he summons his officers to him. The entire regiment is curious and clusters around him. He doesn't send anyone away.

"Gentlemen!" he barks out in his arrogant manner. "There are no Russians in Moscow. The only living beings in the streets are beggars, drunks, and stray dogs. The city is burning. It appears it has been set on fire by Russian agents. The houses and the main stores have been destroyed so that they don't afford us any winter quarters. Napoleon has conquered ruins."

The colonel stops to draw breath. "Gentlemen," he continues. "Unless we set off for home immediately, we are lost. It may be too late as it is. It is to be hoped that Napoleon recognizes the dreadful situation and acts accordingly."

"But will he bite the bullet?" wonders the crestfallen major.

"He has no other choice," says the old staff captain. "The czar wouldn't dream of suing for peace, once he's sacrificed his capital."

The colonel nods, lost in his thoughts.

The old staff captain heaves a sigh that seems to come all the way up from his toe caps.

The night is ghostly and restless. No one sleeps. The whole regiment is mesmerized by the spectacle of such fiendish destruction. The wind drives into the embers and spins them on to intact buildings. One house lights another. Neighbor ignites neighbor. Sheaves of sparks fly up into the black each time a building collapses.

I can't bear to look at the burning city anymore. I feel as though my eyes are burning like the fire in front of me.

23.

Maybe our regiment is the last that still carries out orders. We have been told to go east, to one of the Moscow suburbs, and secure the eastern approaches to the city. But who are we supposed to stop? There are no enemy Russians to be seen anywhere. They have all fled the city, gone to Siberia. Or could it be that they're massing on the other side of the city?

The rest of the *Grande Armée* meets no resistance at all as it enters Moscow from all sides. In wild bunches. There is almost no organization anymore, all forms of obedience have been suspended. The soldiers have turned into treasure seekers and booty hunters. They want to get rich in a hurry, to take as much of it as possible back home with them, so that the war pays off a little bit. They poke around among the scorched and smoking beams, looking for cellar entrances and hidden treasure troves. Clothes and household utensils lie spread out on the streets. The looters are wallowing in flour and sugar and fat, they destroy and spoil everything they can't use or don't want to carry. Only Napoleon's lifeguards preserve discipline. They don't get mixed up in the orgies of destruction. Our colonel grumbles that the Guards aren't interested in small potatoes. They have been shown richer pickings in the Kremlin and in the princely houses around the center.

I see something glittering in the dirt and pick it up. I have never seen anything so precious in my life.

"It's a lady's necklace," says Konrad Klara, and he looks at me strangely, almost a little sadly. I put the thing back down in the dirt.

"As a man, I couldn't very well wear something like that, anyway."

Konrad Klara laughs. It seems to reassure him that I didn't take the jewel.

"There is nothing noble about war," he sighs, and I see his eyes are slightly moist. "The troops forget all their good habits, and turn into thieves. In extremity, a soldier is allowed to requisition food and fodder for his horses. Of course, only with permission. Even if it's just a piece of paper. But that's all right. It's sanctioned by the rights of war. Everything else is theft or brigandage."

I nod. Konrad Klara knows what he's talking about.

Konrad Klara isn't greedy. Is that just because he has

everything he could desire at home, anyway? No, that's certainly not the reason. There are just some people who are different. They always play by the rules, and even in wartime only take as much as they need to live. No more than that.

I wouldn't mind if Konrad Klara really were my brother. Even though it's completely out of the question. Just as out of the question as a common soldier farting on parade.

The weather's looking up: The nights are warmer again. The remains of our regiment aren't required to sleep among smoking and glowing remnants of houses and breathe in the sharp fumes. I've built us a shelter out of tin roofs in a little garden among roses and cabbages. The air there is better.

We are allowed to take turns going into town to look for supplies. There are no more rations and provisioning. It's every man for himself. I look after Konrad Klara. And Konrad Klara looks out for me. He doesn't find it easy, it's true. He comes from a different world. Last night, he told me he's just turned seventeen. So he's just a couple of months older than I am. It's no sort of age to go to war. Anyway, there are enough eatables for ourselves and the two frugal Cossack horses. Every so often, we stumble upon some special delicacy in a store cellar. Then we rejoice and eat like lords.

Occasionally, the colonel is indignant that the lieutenant is still hanging around with Corporal Bayh, instead of hobnobbing in officers' circles where he should be. Seeing as he's descended from a long line of nobles, no doubt going all the way back to some old robber baron. The colonel tells him off for that. Even if the lieutenant doesn't have a command, it's still his responsibility to keep his distance from lower ranks.

The lieutenant count merely smiles and asks his uncle the colonel kindly what he finds so objectionable about Corporal Bayh.

But that's Konrad Klara for you. He's no longer as arrogant as the other officers.

It's one more reason to like him.

The burned and burning streets are destroyed, but they're not dead. At first, I think there must be a lot of Muscovites still in the city. Before long, I notice that that's not it. French and Italians and Portuguese and Westphalians and Prussians and Poles and Wurttemburgers and all the various nationalities from Napoleon's army are doing business, offering plundered or stolen wares for sale or exchange in their various languages. Soldiers have overnight turned into tradesmen. Most of them have new wardrobes. A few are swaggering around in satin and silk, and have the allure of princes or barons.

So the *Grande Armée* is living well in Moscow. A lot of

soldiers have become stinking rich overnight. At least for a few days.

No one needs to go hungry. There are plenty of vegetables in the gardens. Around the city, there are fields full of beets and cabbages. In the ruins, soldiers bake bread and sell it for a ten- or twenty-fold markup.

I don't buy anything, Konrad neither. We don't have any money, seeing as we were plundered bare beside the lake in Borodino. We don't have a penny apiece between us. Even so, we don't go short. Among the wreckage, there are still undiscovered cellars with stores of foodstuffs. And if I fail to find anything one day, then I pilfer from the Wurttemburg and French and Austrian and Saxon traders. I don't see anything wrong with that. The soldiers who have suddenly become wealthy tradesmen only came by their goods in the same way.

24.

After three weeks, our regiment is ordered out. To offer security, apparently. Security for what or whom? Napoleon, who is residing in the Kremlin, waiting for a peace offer to come? Waiting and waiting. Still waiting! How much longer? Till it's too late. This Napoleon doesn't strike me as being terribly clever.

So we withdraw to the edge of the city. Apparently, where there was a German suburb of Moscow, a rich quarter.

The nights have gotten cold again. Konrad Klara finds the buried entrance to a large cellar, where we set up residence. The shelter is warm and dry, and it also contains plenty of provisions. One chest contains a couple of soft fur coats and cases of pistols. Konrad Klara explains that these are dueling pistols. That's what

Russian nobles and officers use to kill each other with, in case one man jolts another or takes a woman away from him. In such cases, you have to insult each other publicly, which leads in turn to a duel. Then the officers and noblemen shoot each other at daybreak. All on account of honor. That's the way things should be, Konrad Klara tells me. They do that in Prussia as well. And with us at home too, but not quite so often.

I feel really fortunate that I'm not a nobleman and don't have to look after my honor. That way no one offends me, and I don't need to be shot in any duel, either.

The furs are clean. We could easily wear them. Thieving? Konrad feels bad. But then he allows me to persuade him that we need something warm to wear. The winter could arrive any day, with ice and snow. If we have the furs, we will survive the great cold. The furs are warm and agreeable to wear. There are no lice or fleas in them, and they don't stink. A louseless fur is a rare commodity in Russia. We give other fur wearers a wide berth. We don't want their populations to move in with us, thank you very much.

The colonel, the major, and the two staff officers are drunk most of the time. They are drowning their rage with Napoleon and his marshals in Russian schnapps. The stuff is called vodka, and it burns like fire all down your insides. My lieutenant doesn't join them. He would rather stay with me, even though I used to be his servant. That's how much he's gotten used to me. Recently, we've been having conversations. Our views aren't all that different on many things. Except for agriculture. He doesn't know the first thing about agriculture. Which is strange, seeing that he has a farm at home that is so big you can't see from one end of it to the other.

One sleepless night, he gets me in a long conversation. He talks about himself, and the world he comes from, his father, his brothers and sisters, and above all his mother. She must be a lovely and wonderful person. Everything revolves around her. There is no one like her in the whole world. Why is he telling me all this, with a childish yearning in his voice? It makes me almost sad. Of course, I'm happy for him that he has such a wonderful mother, but I do feel a little bit envious. Probably Konrad Klara sees the sadness in my face. He looks at me a while, and then suddenly asks me about my mother.

"I haven't much to say on that subject," I reply, as calmly as possible. "Except to bring me into the world, I never had one."

"Oh," sighs Konrad Klara. "That's so terribly sad. But what about your father?"

"I don't have one, either. He was hit by a falling tree, eleven years ago, when he was chopping wood."

"Then you're all alone in the world?"

"No, I've got my farmer. Even though he does peculiar things sometimes." And because Konrad Klara wants
to hear about the farmer, I tell him how I came to be a
soldier at the age of sixteen.

"But that's a scandal!" he bursts out.

"I don't know." I shake my head.

Konrad Klara creases up his brow. He ponders for a
long time. "I expect your farmer is a real pig. Unless I'm
completely mistaken, he's tricked you in the most awful
way. He brought you along to the army, in place of his
own son."

"No! No. That can't be. My farmer's not as cunning
and treacherous as that."

I admit, suspicion has been eating at me for a while
now. At first it was tentative and uncertain, and then it
was like a wicked imp, skipping about between my mind
and my soul. But I was always able to push the horrid
thought away.

Konrad Klara won't let go. He's still thinking about
it. "I'm convinced your farmer is an awful pig, a veritable
devil." He gets really mad. "We're going to have to bring
that criminal to justice. If we get home safely, then I
hope for his sake that God is merciful to him."

Gradually, I start to hate my farmer.

25.

It's halfway through the fourth week in Moscow. A heavy stagecoach emblazoned with a noble coat of arms drives past me. A gentleman is leaning out of the open window, gazing about him in curiosity. No. That's no gentleman. A shock jabs me in the chest like a cold flash of lightning. In spite of his fancy clothes, I recognize him straight away. It's none other than Sergeant Krauter. And something else catches my eye as well. The coach is pulled by the two noble Arab steeds belonging to my lieutenant. What a crime! To use purebred Arabs as draft horses. So Krauter was the robber at the lake by Borodino. Damn it all. That means he also took our money, the rogue.

I try to run after him. But of course his horses, or rather Konrad's, are faster. I wonder if he recognized me?

Rage and thirst for revenge are both banging around in my brain.

In the beginning, Konrad Klara refuses to believe it was Krauter.

"You're seeing things," he says mildly.

But all the same, he spends the next few days combing the whole quarter with me. We find no trace of the horses and the villain. He must have some good hideaway. Sometimes I have really peculiar thoughts. For instance, that Krauter is no ordinary sergeant. More, that he's no ordinary human being. Perhaps he's the devil himself.

26.

The lieutenant is summoned by the regimental commander.

No, he's not getting a platoon. There are almost no men and horses left. Who or what would he be given to command, if there's nothing left to command, except himself and me?

Instead, he comes back with news.

Odd rumors are blowing back and forth through the *Grand Armée.* Changing all the time. According to one, the czar wants peace, but Napoleon has rejected his offer. Another rumor has it exactly the other way around. Napoleon is waiting for the Russians to capitulate, but of course the czar intends no such thing.

The lieutenant says what the colonel thinks about these rumors. According to him, Napoleon is trembling with rage. He is still waiting impatiently for the czar finally to surrender. The czar has to. If he doesn't, it flies in the face of the whole etiquette of war. After all, his capital city has been taken. The colonel has also heard that there are some French scouts bringing reports of a large Russian army advancing from the south.

"Thunder and lightning!" he exclaimed, according to the lieutenant. "May God be merciful to us! If we don't pull out in time, it'll be all up with us." And then the colonel grunted crossly: "In any case, there is no *Grande Armée* that's fit to give battle anymore. And the Russian winter is advancing upon us. It will be there, just as sure as our tiny horses drop tiny balls of dung. In addition to ferocious cold, the winter will bring such masses of snow that a man will be crushed flat unless he finds shelter in time. Winter comes with sudden speed in these parts. Overnight, even."

That's what the colonel said, and my lieutenant passed it on. And the colonel knows what he is talking about. As a young captain, he spent a few summers and winters in the service of the czar. Then my lieutenant says that the colonel muttered to himself: "Maybe Napoleon's lost his marbles? If he can't bring about peace, then he needs to turn back and make for home with all speed. What else is he waiting for? For the ruination of himself and of us all?"

That's pretty much what Konrad Klara thinks too, and I have no option but to take a similar view myself. What else are we waiting for, in this inhospitable country?

The days are getting colder. There's snow in the air, still shrouded in heavy gray clouds. Woe betide those it falls on! For the moment, it's still hanging above us. But already you can smell it.

Napoleon has suddenly surfaced. He calls his *Grande Armée* together. With the last bit of ceremonial hoo-ha, he holds a troop inspection outside the gates of Moscow. He inspects the miserable remnants with no expression on his face. There are still a few officers and men who believe in the possibility of victory.

"Vive l'Empereur!" they cry out lustily and respectfully.

The same day, Napoleon orders the retreat from Moscow.

Apparently, it is the 18th of October.

"Thunder and lightning! It's far too late!" barks the colonel, and the officers agree with him.

The following morning, at three o'clock sharp, what's left of the once so proud *Grande Armée* moves out. The tattered regiments are no longer recognizable as they trudge back along the battered roads. Decaying bodies, heroes of the invasion, are still littered around the outskirts of Moscow. No one has taken the time to bury the shot-up bodies in the ground.

We must hurry home. And quickly. Before the Russians cut off our escape route and before the winter comes.

Our regiment pulls out with the others. Some marshal of Napoleon's gives the orders. We are assigned to cover the rear of the *Grande Armée*. Ahead of us are choked highways, and left and right is devastated, empty, starved country, and behind us are swarms of Cossacks and sometimes armed peasant bands.

At least we're going in the right direction.

I wonder if we'll ever get home?

But Napoleon is still in charge. He orders everything that stands to be destroyed. "All food for man and beast — nothing must fall into the hands of the enemy."

And so we pour brandy and beer and other good things into the dirt, mixing them with flour and fat and oats. All these things, suddenly gone to waste. When whole regiments had to starve, previously. Apparently, it is on Napoleon's orders that the Kremlin, seat of the czars, has been blown up as well.

Another one of Napoleon's orders is addressed to regimental commanders. The retreat is to follow a southerly direction. There is still peaceful terrain there, offering enough food for man and horse. Possibly even a secure winter quarters.

The colonel is getting nervous. "Thunder and lightning! South, ha? That would be nice!"

There are powerful Russian units to the south. Kutusov himself, the stubborn Russian commander-in-chief, is at their head. He comes between the *Grande Armée* and the route to the untouched territories to the south. To engage the powerful enemy is out of the question. Kutusov forces Napoleon back along the same way he came. And that's ravaged and deserted. There is no more food there for man or beast, no shelter, no protection from the cold. Only burned-out towns and villages and moldering corpses lining the route.

Hunger and thirst accompany the defeated army.

Behind some bushes, Konrad Klara finds a hidden market garden with a bed of beets and onions. Better than nothing.

Command from a general: "All horses are to be given in! The last two howitzers need draft horses."

So we're on foot once more. Step by step. We throw away everything we don't absolutely need. We can't be lugging useless weight with us. The furs are bothersome. They weigh down on our weak, hungry bodies. But what happens when the big freeze comes that everyone is talking about? Then the furs might save our lives. So we keep the weight and drag it along with us.

Carriages overtake us, weighed down with trophies and junk and everything the heart desires, or greed demands, or that promises wealth.

A chaise with a noble coat of arms drives by. That's the conveyance in which Sergeant Krauter rode through Moscow. Terror swirls in my veins. Konrad Klara starts to tremble as well. He has spotted his noble Arab steeds. "Stop!" he cries out. "Stop that swindler! He's stolen my horses." But no one takes any notice. A few soldiers nearby look contemptuously at the Portuguese lieutenant who speaks German. In Saxon dialect, someone says to him: "Don't fancy walking anymore, eh? But if you want a horse, you'll have to come up with something better than that old trick." For a while, I run along behind the droshky. I almost catch it. I just need to hop up on the running board.

"You wretch!" I call out to the man on the box. He reaches for his whip and smashes me across the face. The sergeant sticks his head out the window. A woman lifts her face from his shoulder and looks at me in astonishment. "Hey!" Krauter calls out to his coachman. "Isn't that our transport soldier running along after us?"

"Yes!" shouts the one on top. "That's the idiot from my village!"

I stagger and fall. The following marchers step on me. Luckily, Konrad Klara comes along, pulls me to my feet, and drags me back into the moving stream of fugitives. The droshky is out of sight. Other conveyances with noble personages roll by. They've probably come straight from Moscow. Packed full of riches.

"Please give us a morsel of bread!" beg the tired soldiers. But no one glances at them. The elegant carriages drive past in a hurry, followed by a whole train of baggage.

On the street lies an upset barrel. Thousands of kopek pieces have spilled onto the dirt. What riches! But no one is interested. If only it were bread. What would we do with metal coin? There's nothing to buy with it, and money would only weigh us down.

Winter announces itself. At first, with cold, steady rain. Knee-deep mud mires all the roads. The army is stuck in the sludge, and our feet are glued to the road. Droshkies and baggage carts lie by the roadside, stranded and looted. They are no more good for anything. The wheels are unable to cut through the morass.

Only a hard frost can overcome the mud and make the roads once more passable for foot and horse and carriage. Maybe that would be the lesser evil. We long for the feared cold to come.

Cossacks and Bashkirs and Lord knows what kind of Russians ride up from the side, hew and smite, and disappear. Any of the *Grande Armée* who try to avoid the muddy highway are cut to ribbons.

How far is it to Smolensk? And how much farther home? There is said to be food in Smolensk. Huge store-houses full of it. I wonder if it's true? We can't trust all the things we're told. We've been getting it from the wrong end of the horse too many times.

28.

On one of the last days of October, there it is suddenly: the longed-for and long-dreaded frost. Overnight, an icy east wind freezes the mud to rock. Almost simultaneously, the heavy black clouds discharge their burdens.

Now it's just as well we've held on to our furs. The first cold snowy night we have to spend out of doors. Far and wide, there's only one single wooden structure. Which is full to the last inch. The men are even lying on top of each other.

"Let us in!"

"What have you got to pay with? Food? Vodka? Nothing? Then there's no room. You can see for yourselves."

Beside the road, we lay one fur down on the snow, and then we cover ourselves up with the other one. We exhale our own warmth into the gap. Snow is still falling. It packs, insulates, warms. So we manage to survive half the night. Then I feel someone tugging at our top fur. I wake up in time and shoo away the thief. There's no more hope of sleep. Beside us someone is lying there half-naked. He doesn't stir. Frozen. Was he stripped first, or was he already dead when they stole his clothes?

Konrad Klara weeps to himself. His tears freeze on his cheeks.

"Come on, Konrad Klara. We must move on."

"What about our regiment?"

"I can't see anyone. Probably the regiment doesn't exist anymore."

The street is still almost empty. Nothing is coming from Moscow now. Either the fugitives are asleep under the snow, or else they've already frozen to death. In the dawn, Konrad Klara sees a young man in a thin French uniform leaning against a birch.

"Hey, you! You'll freeze if you stay there."

The young man doesn't stir. He must have fallen asleep with exhaustion. I tramp over to him to shake him awake. I'm too late. He is stiff as a wooden beam. Konrad Klara wipes his eyes. Is my pity already frozen? It only pipes up very feebly.

The days are dark, the nights clear and icy. On the side of the road are cannons stuck in the snow. They've gone as far as they can go. They've been nailed up. There are no more commands and no more organization. Who would go to the trouble of lugging cannons around anymore? Everyone just wants to save his own life. Rifles are tossed into the snow. A thin branch, a half-charred beam, a bundle of straw are all more use. They offer the chance to be admitted to a campfire site at night. A fire that would save a person from freezing.

We must have something like a guardian angel, Konrad Klara and I. Through the blizzard we spot a dark stain some little way off the road. A barn? Or something better still? We should have a look. We haven't been attacked by Cossacks for a whole day now. It's not a great risk, then. We leave the road and stamp through the loose snowdrifts. We're wallowing about up to our chests. What it is is a baggage cart. The wind cleared the snow from the top of it. That was the dark thing we spotted from the road. With our bare hands, we dig our way into the cart. What wonders! Frozen bread and lard are in there. Hopefully, no one has seen us. Having something like that could be fatal for us.

But now we have food again. We stash it under our fur coats.

At night, we leave the road a few paces, dig a hollow in the snow, and bury ourselves in it in our furs. One underneath, one on top, a little snow over that. Our own warmth stays in.

Young Alsatian soldiers, aged sixteen or thereabouts, come out to meet us. They are Napoleon's last throw. They have just gotten here, and take over the rear guard from us. They are desperate to fight. There's nothing we can do for them. I wonder how long they're going to live?

The snow lets up, but it gets colder.

"I'm not going to make it home," Konrad Klara sighs to himself.

"What are you doing, spouting such nonsense?"

"Just talking."

"No, come on. Spit it out. Is something hurting you?"

"No. Not really. But I saw the black butterflies last night."

"You saw what? Black butterflies? In the middle of winter? With this cold?"

"Not really. In my sleep, you know. I saw Sergeant Krauter as well."

"Oh, I see. Do you have any idea of the stuff I dream? Lots of nonsense. I expect the butterflies were brown, you just didn't see the colors clearly. And Krauter, that bastard, he can't do anything to us as long as we stick together. Together, we're stronger than he is. Let's not think about him anymore."

Konrad Klara's eyes brighten.

"You're right!" he says, sounding slightly calmer. "Nothing can happen to us. Fortune favors us. And together we're going to make it back."

177

Even the sun comes out. Admittedly, it doesn't succeed in making the air any warmer. Our breath freezes in front of our faces. The following night is the coldest of all. We dig our sleeping place deep into the snow on the edge of a forest. A few twigs underneath and over us to keep our body heat in the hole. During the night, thousands freeze.

Smolensk is a huge disappointment. There is nothing left to eat there. The Imperial Guards have emptied out the storehouses. They've lived like maggots in bacon, they're full to bursting, and now they're on their way home with Napoleon their emperor. That's the rumor. Truth or lie.

The fury of the troops following after is indescribable.

Konrad Klara breaks down and cries again. Tears of rage, this time.

29.

It's a particularly nasty day in late November. Cannons are thumping ahead of us and behind us and either side of the marching route. Rifle fire is crackling very nearby. Step-by-step, the men shuffle along in the thousandfold tracks left in the snow.

At around midday, the procession suddenly grinds to a halt. It gets going again with curses. Beyond the edge of the highway, the surface of the snow has been smashed. Cannonballs have plowed through it. There are corpses lying among wrecked baggage carts. No one notices them. Probably a surprise attack from Cossacks and artillery. Four mortally wounded horses are twitching in their death agonies. Men are hunkered around them, cutting into the steaming bodies. Others are tearing off cartwheels and planks and feeding them to a fire.

We join them and help. No one minds. There's

enough meat after all, four whole horses. That's enough for a lot of people. But not for long. More soldiers keep turning up. The scent draws them. Food! More and more hungry men huddle around the fire. They reach forward into the embers to grab at morsels. Those sitting at the front are knocked over. Oaths and shouts.

I fish out a couple of pieces of meat from the embers, shove them under my fur coat, and then drag Konrad Klara away from the fire. A few elbows to left and right, and we're clear of the crowd. We walk on, and before long we find a quieter place, where we gulp down our still warm pieces of horseflesh. A little strength returns to our tired bodies.

Shortly thereafter we see the horrible end of Hanselmann, the son of the Schonbronn cobbler. He was the cannoneer who always followed Sergeant Krauter around. He's lying in some dark red snow. A cannonball tore off his lower limbs. He didn't stand a chance against a direct hit like that. There's nothing left for the surgeon to stitch there. I feel sad, even though Hanselmann hit me across the face with a whip only a couple of days ago. It didn't have to be such a big cannonball as that. The sergeant isn't there. It seems he's managed to get away once more.

Toward evening of that same day, a sleigh forces its way with loud whip cracking and shouts through the men trudging along. There are four men in furs seated on it.

"Ho, you!" one of them calls out, and the sleigh brakes. "Thunder and lightning! Aren't you young Count Lammersdorf?"

Konrad Klara perks up. Thunder and lightning? His uncle, the colonel, always said that. O terror! O joy! So the colonel's still alive.

The colonel orders him without much hoo-ha to hop in and turns to ask the bundle of fur beside him: "Your Excellency surely won't mind if we take along my nephew? If we squeeze together, there's enough room."

A great man, that uncle. What a turnup! That's how quickly things can change, from one second to the next. It's good for Konrad Klara and for me. Suddenly, we have a little more future to look forward to. The stomping through the snow is over for now. We can save our strength. I'm sure the gentlemen will have something that Konrad Klara and I can eat as well. And the sleigh covers the ground much faster than our dog-tired legs. Suddenly, home has moved considerably nearer.

Joyfully, the lieutenant leaps up onto the sleigh and squeezes into the seat beside his uncle.

"Adam Neve! Come along! Hop on board!"

"Hold on!" the uncle butts in. "We don't have that much room!"

"But can't Adam Neve sit on me, or the other way round?" begs Konrad Klara.

"Thunder and lightning! Who is this Adam Neve? Another young lieutenant?"

"No, uncle! He's the corporal! You remember the one, my former servant!"

"Well, I'm afraid we can't have that. We don't have room for any servants here. You have to come on your own. Alone. No one with you."

The mass of men on the road is pushing and surging. I am picked up by it and pushed past the sleigh. I feel utterly miserable, my head is empty, I am incapable of thought.

The Excellency in the sleigh orders crossly: "Onward!"

The horses pull. Cracks of the whip and shouts clear a space for the sleigh.

Then Konrad Klara jumps off.

"Not without him," he calls out to the colonel, waves to him, and is once again trudging at my side on the snow-covered marching route.

"Thunder and lightning!" the colonel shouts back to his nephew. Along with something else, which is swallowed up by his fur collar.

Tangles of thoughts bounce back and forth in my head. What should I say? Konrad Klara has turned down the comfortable offer of rescue. On my account. I wipe my nose several times. I need to too, because the damned cold at nightfall freezes everything on the spot.

30.

Each time a horse collapses, soldiers fall on it, beat and fight one another for it, and hack off pieces for themselves. There's not usually much meat to be had. The animals are mostly skin and bone. But that's worth something, too. More than nothing.

How much farther is it home?

But we're lucky. We're still alive. And healthy. We haven't even got frostbite on our fingers and toes. Usually, we have a little something to eat. What more could we wish for? Sometimes we walk half the night. That gives us a little edge. At night, the road is almost empty. By day, it's only the Imperial Guards who are ahead of us, a few half-preserved regiments, maybe Poles, who are reasonably well armed, and some like us, who want to stick close to the Guards because they keep the swirling bands of Cossacks at bay. There is reported to be a Wurttemburg regiment there as well.

Behind us comes the hungry, demoralized mass of the defeated *Grande Armée*. That's where chaos is.

From time to time, we find a bit of wood or something eatable off the road.

A calf lies buried in snow next to a well. Konrad Klara notices the hump in the snow. It seems he has a nose for buried treasure. The calf smells clean and innocent. It froze quickly and thoroughly.

Not far off are some priests sitting around a campfire. Trustworthy-looking men. At least they seem peaceful enough. A few pieces of wood lying nearby give promise of a warm night. They haven't anything to eat. At least, I can't see any evidence that they do. That's good for us. On account of the calf.

The men aren't priests at all. They're from a regiment of Badensers. They've stolen the priestly robes from a church. Because of the cold. All's well in cold and war. Who can blame them? It turns into a wonderful night. Only a pity there's no salt to put in the broth and on the roast veal.

We sleep into the early morning hours around the hospitable fire. We feel much better. It's good to know there are decent people, even among the rough, neglected soldiers. The ostensible priests round the campfire are an example of such. They only steal Konrad's knife, not our furs or our boots, which we need to live. They even have a present for us. Overnight some of those little creatures that tickle their possessor with bites and suck his blood have crept into our furs.

The days and nights are indistinguishable. They take place on and close to the marching route. With a little luck, there's some horse meat, warm snow water, and a little fire for the night. And our boots are holding up. So we don't often suffer from wet feet.

It turns warm again overnight. Snow turns to slush, and our feet move slowly and heavily through it.

More pressure on us from the Russians. Cossacks are now hovering around the broken *Grande Armée*, incessantly and mercilessly setting about its poor remnants. Only the Imperial Guards and a few fresh Polish regiments can still make a stand.

Suddenly, the fugitive stream stops. We hear violent thunder of cannons. A wrecked town. There's no way through. Impacts from howitzer balls. Terrified crowds of men washing this way and that.

Konrad's uncle and the Excellency are caught up in the chaos in their sleigh. So they haven't gotten any farther ahead than we have. There's no way forward and no way back.

"Thunder and lightning!" curses the colonel. "There

you are again." Konrad Klara fights his way toward his uncle with knees, elbows, and feet. There's no way through. The frightened horses are lashing out. Men are shouting and pushing and trying to get through the crush of people. The colonel is just getting up to try to force his way over to his nephew when the ball strikes. It wrecks the sleigh, the horses, and the fur-wrapped Excellency.

We are terrified.

Konrad Klara vaults over corpses and screaming wounded. His uncle is past help. His shattered legs are lying beside him. But he takes his time dying.

"Thunder and lightning!" he says to his nephew. "That had to have been a seven-pounder at least! Well, at this point I'm handing in my commission!"

And that's it.

Konrad Klara is weeping again. Even though he never particularly liked his uncle.

He was born with a soft heart. It will never be hard.

31.

The fleeing army is stopped again. No getting through.

"Beresina's in the way!"

"What, a woman?"

"No, of course not."

"The Beresina's a wide-ish river. There are apparently no more bridges across it. The Russians have burned them all."

"We'll be pretty safe when we're on the other side."

"Well then, let's get across!"

"How do you propose to do that?"

"Over the ice!"

"The ice is too thin. It's already cracked."

"Then there's nothing for it but to build bridges!"

"That's what they're trying to do. If the Russians will allow."

"We'll have to hold them off that long."

"Napoleon's seeing what he can do. He needs to get across himself. Apparently, he's leading the Russians a dance. He's distracting them with a false maneuver and is secretly building a couple of bridges. Right here."

"He'd better be quick about it, then, before the Russian army gets here. The first of them are already up there, with a couple of cannons. Once they find their range . . ."

This, more or less, is the conversation of a couple of ragged Saxon officers.

From up on a hilltop, the Russians are shelling us with heavy howitzers.

Konrad Klara and I have crept under a fir tree. We press ourselves against the trunk. Konrad Klara is listening to the Saxons' conversation. He can't understand everything they say. French would be easier for him. The officers pull in their heads. A cannonball digs a big hole nearby. The Russians have a good view of everything. They shoot at anything that moves. No one stops them. It's just as well we're standing under the shelter of a tree.

We try to make ourselves as small as we can.

"If only we were already on the other side!" repeats one of the Saxons. And he sighs with deep longing.

"I've been told by a general," another fellow pops up self-importantly, "that the Russians are coming up with fresh troops. They want to cut off Napoleon's escape route. They want to trap him here on the Beresina and finish him off. For good."

Another hole. Very close. The Russians are getting in range of the tree. Perhaps they suspect Napoleon is hiding under it?

We run off. By various detours, we find ourselves down by the river. Things are quieter down here. We're out of range of the cannons, for a start. Also, the men fleeing from the Russians aren't milling about down here, but over where the bridges are going up. They want to get across fast, if the bridges hold.

"Beresina's a nice name."

"But its water is deep and icy cold."

A mild spell of weather has softened the ice and made it impassable. There are some who would rather not believe it. A few daredevils keep trying their luck and plunge into the icy cold. They grab hold of beams and boards, and try to swim across. Most don't even get halfway. There the current grabs them, and they vanish between the blocks of ice.

Upstream, Napoleon's engineers are working on the bridges. The very last remnants of the *Grande Armée* are backed up nearby. They're waiting impatiently for the crossings to be finished. They are unable to go forward or back, and fresh arrivals keep coming. The Russians are on a slope to the east and shelling the mass of men with cannons and howitzers. It's an unfair, one-sided battle.

And on the other side is safety. Probably.

Where is Napoleon? He and his Guards must still be on this side. Apparently, he's taken personal charge of the bridge-building. I hope they'll be finished soon. I'm sure he'll be the first to safety.

As for the others, I wonder how many of us will make it? The Russians will quickly get in range of the bridges. The earlier you go, the better your chances.

A troop of French rides along the bank. Elegant and proud. As if it were maneuvers in peacetime. I wonder if they're Imperial Guards? Surely. There aren't many other such fine-looking troops left. They're up to something. Aha, they want to mount a flank attack on the hill with the Russian howitzers. To take them from the back.

That's a daring move. But absolutely necessary. The cannons are disrupting the bridge-building. They pull off their risky maneuver. The Russians are so surprised that they abandon their cannons and run off. But before the French can spike all the guns, a group of Cossacks gallops up and drives them back. Four or five of the Guards are hacked to pieces with sabers. Their riderless horses run with the others for a while. Then they drift off, trot now here, now there, and then come to a stop.

Magnificent horses.

"If we had those!" My heart is beating up into my head. "Look at them."

The same idea has occurred to Konrad Klara.

"Come on! We'll catch them."

Other men have also spotted the horses. They run up to them from several sides.

As if by miracle, we manage. Or is it that horses just like me? Who knows. At any rate, they walk trustingly up to me. We quickly select the two best-looking ones. Then we're up in the saddle. We ride back and forth a little, to introduce ourselves to the animals.

A triumph.

"And now we're off!"

"The only thing left to wish for now is that we belonged to the Imperial Guards," says Konrad. "Then we'd have a good chance of being among the first to cross the bridge with Napoleon."

"But we're not in the Guards."

"Well, you're almost French. At least you're wearing a French uniform."

"But you're not," I reflect. "And I'm not going any- where without you."

"Here's a thought!" exclaims Konrad Klara. "There are some dead Frenchmen up by the cannons. With nice uniforms. We just need a cap and a cloak apiece."

There's nothing left to think about. We chase up the

hill in a mad gallop. The Russian cannoneers are just returning to their cannons. They don't pay any attention to two horsemen. They've got both hands full with their cannons. They're so dead set on destroying the bridge, it's for us to take advantage.

Now to the dead Frenchmen! We can't bring ourselves to take off their cloaks. But a couple of caps are lying there. We pick them up, and quickly ride off.

32.

The first bridge is completed.

A mob of men is milling around in front of it. Sounds of cornets. The Guards assemble. With their horses and sabers, they clear space for themselves. They bodily push back the other fugitives. Some cannons and a few intact Polish units are all they permit to come up alongside themselves.

Now's the time.

We force our way through the crowd on horseback, counting on the fear and respect for the Guards. I hope we're right. Yes, the men shrink back. Our Guards' caps work wonders.

Konrad is nervous. If we don't make it through the crowd on time and meet up with the Guards, then we're done for. Only with Napoleon and his mighty Guards do we have a chance of getting safely across, with luck. As individuals, we're powerless. No one would respect us. Maybe we would even fall victim to the rage and resentment of the crowd.

There. The first of the Guards is riding over the bridge. This is it! Just as well that Konrad Klara speaks French. He swears and scolds the men at the top of his voice. I copy him, but while the sounds I make don't sound German, they don't sound particularly French, either. Still, they do the trick. A narrow channel clears in front of us. Slowly, we push our way along. The Russians are getting in range of the new bridge. For the moment, the cannonballs are either dropping into the Beresina, or else smashing into the waiting crowds. But for how much longer? Soon, they'll strike the bridge. Konrad Klara is yelling and swearing. We're almost there. It's not much farther. I can already hear the clatter of hooves on the planks. A carriage rattles past, probably with Napoleon in it. Or maybe he's not, and it's just a clever decoy. It could be that the emperor's in an ordinary uniform and riding somewhere in the midst of his Guards. Everything's possible. The pressure around the bridge gets stronger all the time. The Guards won't be able to hold the others back for very much longer.

"*Attendez! He!*" We wave our Guards' caps and yell. At last someone notices us. Of course, the French take us for a couple of tardy fellows from the regiment, who like to cut things fine. They ride up to us with sabers drawn.

So we manage to get to the bridge in time and cross the Beresina with Napoleon's Guards.

On the eastern side of the river, there are now the most indescribable scenes. Once the Guards have passed, the military police who were keeping order at the bridge-head are simply thrown into the river. The hemmed-in crowd surges onto the narrow crossing. Everyone wants to be the first to get across. There's the most ruthless pushing and shoving to get onto the boards. Anyone who loses his footing is lost. He's simply trampled underfoot and ends up in the river. Whoever's pushed to the side of the bridge falls in. The screams of the crushed and drowning men mingle with pitiful prayers, with curses, and with the crashes of the Russian artillery. Konrad Klara slumps on his horse in horror. He keeps wiping his eyes with his sleeve. Is he trying to brush away the hateful scenes? We have never seen the like. It's an absolute hell on earth.

Many thousands are drowning in the icy cold waters. The Russian gunnery is getting closer and closer to the bridge.

We are among the lucky ones who are riding away from the war with Napoleon.

To freedom.

Or so we think.

There are no Russian troops on this side of the Beresina. Not yet. They're busy surrounding the rest of the fleeing *Grande Armée* on the opposite side and destroying them. We hear the banging of their cannons for a long time to come.

It turns colder again. Arctic cold from Siberia displaces the warm air of the last three days. It's still only the beginning of December. It's just as well we didn't throw away our fur coats.

The Guards are in a tearing rush. They want to be in Vilnius in five days. Vilnius is the only large-sized town with a regular French garrison. A town with every amenity, with proper billets and full storehouses.

The first chance we have, we part company with the French. Before the Guards notice the deception. They didn't notice anything yet. Konrad warns me not to open my mouth. I'm to point to my mouth and mime dumbness. Konrad speaks French. At home, he speaks more French than German. As is the way with the aristocracy. Particularly when there are visitors, the style is French and cultured. I am proud of him.

We slip away into the darkness, without having seen the great Napoleon. A pity, but then again, never mind! The Guards don't notice our disappearance. They are distracted by the cold. They are riding out in all directions, looking for bits of wood. They take everything they find. They drag whole houses along after them. They tie the beams to their horses, and drag them across the snow back to their campsite.

We join a group of Prussians. We have to join someone. Our own regiment no longer exists. The last of them must have drowned in the Beresina. The Prussians have had it up to here with Napoleon. Their officers wish him to the devil. They don't want to die for that madman. Well-mounted and reasonably well-armed, they are heading for Vilnius. They avoid larger troops of Cossacks, while smaller units or bands of armed peasants steer clear of them in turn. But the Prussians have one great disadvantage. Their uniforms are no good in the cold. Napoleon was only planning on a brief summer campaign, and the Prussians left too late to get warm clothing. They don't want civilian gear. That doesn't go with the Prussian pride in their uniform. On cold nights, they shelter in remote villages or farmhouses. There's usually a bit of wood there for a fire. That way, they and we are spared more casualties from frostbite. As long as there's a fire going.

But the war isn't over yet. It follows us wherever we go.

Whoever thought that by crossing the Beresina, we

would be over the worst was in for a big disappointment. Kutusov himself, the tough Russian marshal, has crossed the Beresina and set off after the vanquished army with a huge force. There is no time to rest or linger.

We, too, need to get our skates on. The Prussians are too slow for us. Every night, they spend a long time looking for warmth and shelter. But there is almost nothing to be had. The whole region has been burned and destroyed, and firewood is becoming increasingly scarce. But without fire, the Prussians are doomed. The cold puts a merciless end to any life. The Prussian captain is freezing the most. He doesn't show it, but I see him secretly eyeing Konrad's fur and mine. We really have to be on the lookout.

On our second night with the Prussians, I have an awful nightmare. Krauter has turned up again. Unbelievable! That fiend is standing with a horrible smirk right in the middle of the campfire and extinguishing it with his piss. And suddenly it turns icy cold. So cold that even my thick fur coat no longer warms me. If I am cold, then Konrad Klara beside me must be cold as well. A violent rage shakes me. I want to hurl myself at Krauter, that miscreant! Then I wake up. Krauter isn't pissing on the fire, because Krauter isn't there. But it's still cold. Very cold. And no wonder — the fire's gone out. The sentry went to sleep and didn't keep the fire banked up with wood. I blow on the embers. Except for a few pathetic sparks, too weak to light anything, the fire's gone cold. No, there in one corner is a last glowing core. Konrad crawls out of his fur. Together, we puff on the few remaining embers, urging them to catch again. With a lot of effort and persuasion, a little warmth spreads to the sleeping Prussians. But the warmth causes no stir of life. Only the captain still moves, sits up, and stares in front of him. The others remain rigid. They won't be thawed out. No — one suddenly leaps up and stomps out into the night, screaming. He must have lost his mind. He doesn't return.

33.

After four days, we are in Vilnius. The French have already gone, the storehouses are empty, and the local population hostile. Anything the Guards didn't take with them, the inhabitants helped themselves to. Only people with a great deal of money can afford to buy anything. And we don't have any money.

After one night trembling with cold under the city walls, our horses are gone. The leather harness with which we tied them up was cut. Our fur coats weren't taken, though. The following day, we slip into a little hut in an outlying district. The old woman inside takes pity on us poor young fellows. It's reasonably warm in the hut, and we have a lot of sleep to catch up on. After two days, the old woman wakes us. She gestures animatedly with her hands and feet, and explains that the advance guard of the Russian army is already moving into the other end of the town. It's high time we fled.

But already it's too late. The Cossacks have ringed the city. All loopholes are closed. Vilnius has become a trap. Its buildings are full of sick and mangled soldiers. Before they left, the French forced the townspeople to billet their wounded. Now, the citizens are getting their own back. The sick and injured French are simply pushed out of doors and windows. The misery is indescribable.

We have burned our Guards' hats. We know from hearsay that there is no love lost between the Cossacks and the French. There never was much to begin with, and then there's the matter of Moscow. In the eyes of the Russians, Napoleon is responsible for the destruction of their beloved capital. It doesn't therefore seem advisable to us to be caught wearing the hated uniform.

The old woman is like a kind grandmother. She provides us with shirts, trousers, and tunics. All of them too small. Maybe she once had sons or grandsons whom these things fitted. The trousers end just below my knees. So the old woman wraps linen rags around our bare legs. We look like a couple of dirty urchins sitting with the woman as the Cossacks search the house, looking for enemies. They don't find anything in the poor wooden hut to cause them to suspect. The poverty is too glaring, and the pair of us don't look to them like enemy soldiers.

Just as well the Cossacks either didn't spot or didn't think about the fur coats. Then they would have realized that they don't belong in such a place.

We feel well guarded and sheltered with our Russian grandmother.

The world is mad. Things happen that you wouldn't have believed possible.

Suddenly, they're back. Konrad's noble Arab horses. Unmistakable! They gallop past the entrance to the hut. This time they're harnessed to a sleigh. They're haring out of Vilnius. The sleigh has one single occupant. Krauter! It's bound to be. He lashes out at the horses with his whip. From time to time, he cranes his neck to look behind him. And now we see why the sleigh is being driven at such speed. A band of Cossacks is at his heels, the distance between them diminishing steadily. Slowly but surely, they're gaining on him. Closer to him all the time.

We watch the chase excitedly. "This is it for him!" I say. "I hope they get him." It sounds very spiteful, and I mean it too. I don't care what happens to Krauter. Konrad Klara adds in sorrowful tones: "This is it for my horses as well."

In wild pursuit, they race across the white expanse outside the city. The sleigh in front, and the Cossacks behind.

A few of the Cossacks have overtaken Krauter now.

Probably they want to head him off. They're almost successful in that too. But the sleigh charges on. The horses are whipped. The advantage grows again. It's a splendid and knuckle-whitening spectacle. A real contest.

"My horses," says Konrad Klara, not sure whether to be proud or to lament. The Cossacks don't give up. Once again, they close in on the sleigh. Very close! They have Krauter in a pincer movement. This time he won't get away.

"Bravo!" I call out.

"For shame . . ." mourns Konrad Klara.

A dusting of snow from the other side. A troop of horsemen. The horses bigger. Not Russians, for sure. Are there any more well-armed French units around?

"Poles!" says Konrad Klara.

The Cossacks veer off. Probably they don't want to get in a fight over one sleigh. Most likely, they're going back for reinforcements. That'll take a while. By the time they've arrived, it will all be over. The Poles and the sleigh with Krauter in it move slowly along the horizon, a sprinkling of dots. They won't be caught.

Konrad Klara is happy that his horses have managed to get away from the Cossacks. He doesn't even mind that Krauter gave them the slip. He probably doesn't have it in him to really hate someone. Not even Krauter. I'm disappointed.

34.

Vilnius is sealed, the Russians are letting no one in and no one out. For the moment, we're not in danger. But how long will that be the case? It can change from one day to the next. The old woman won't betray us or throw us out, but we're going to have to live off something. We have no supplies, and we can't buy anything, either. The little that the nice old granny has we mustn't continue to eat up.

Twice already we've tried to get out and promptly turned back. No success. The Russians are mounting patrols round the clock. There are no gaps and no way through. Not at night, even. For the past few nights, the sky has been clear and bright, and the moon about twice as big as we'd wish it to be, shining on the snowy fields around the city. There's no way we can sneak out across them. Any sign of life on that paper-white surface will be detected right away. We need fast horses to get us out of the city.

We ponder the various possibilities. What can we do to get food for ourselves? Work? Without knowledge of Russian? That won't be possible. We'd be identified right away as enemies in hiding or — even worse — as spies. That would be the end. Begging? But most people have nothing here themselves, and the ones that do don't give to beggars. There's only stealing left.

"Not again," moans Konrad Klara. "I don't hold with stealing. I'd rather starve!"

"So the little blue blood is too delicate to steal," I sneer. "Well, where else are we going to get anything from? What are we going to live off? We'll just go under."

"What did you call me? Blue blood?"

"Yes, blue blood!" I repeat crossly.

Whereupon one word leads to another, and for the first time there's a big silence between us. All day long we don't talk to each other. We avoid each other, insofar as that's possible in a not very big hut. By late evening, we've used up our ill temper. We're getting along again. And then we head out together to steal bread, beets, or whatever it might be. One of us goes here, the other there. We both come home empty-handed. It appears that stealing under such difficult circumstances is something that requires practice. Konrad Klara seems not to have any talent for it at all, and I'm not that good, either. Vilnius has been picked clean, and those people that have anything at all guard their possessions more closely than they would their souls. There's nothing left for simple thieves.

What now?

"We have to get out of Vilnius."

"Definitely."

"But how?"

The old woman senses our perplexity. She furrows her already creased brow a little more, reflects a little, and then with her mouth and her feet, she makes the clopping sound of horses. Because we look at her doubtfully, with her right hand she makes the apparently international mime for theft.

Brief reflection.

"Fine, but?"

"Of course! We have to steal horses."

Luckily, it seems horses are more plentiful in Vilnius than unattached loaves of bread. In stables, sheds, barns, outhouses, even under lean-tos, there they are. The city is full of Cossack and other Russian cavalry regiments. There are even more horses than turnips.

Konrad Klara has no objection to this type of theft. It's not crime, to his way of seeing it, but an act of war. We would merely be confiscating enemy soldiers' horses. No dishonor attaches to that.

On the same night, we try to break out. It's not quite as bright as previously. The moon is behind clouds, so the snow is a little less luminous, though for our purposes it still looks pretty bright. Anyway — it's either or. We don't have any other choice. With heavy hearts, we eat with the old woman one more time. Some grain porridge and a piece of bread. Then we kiss her on both cheeks. Like a mother.

We find a couple of good horses, not far away. They're standing in an open paddock. It's easy to lead them out. There's a big bundle of hay in front of them, so they're not going to be hungry, either. They've already had their dinner. That's good, because who knows when they'll get their next meal. We can't see any saddles. Too bad. But it would be dangerous to hunt around for too long. Any moment, someone could come out to see to them and catch us.

I take the smaller of them. I talk to it softly and soothingly. Then I try out the seat. As a boy, I often rode bareback. Konrad Klara doesn't find it quite so easy. He's only ever had saddled horses between his thighs. But he can manage, too.

We ride cautiously to the edge of town. A patrol is just galloping past. The Cossacks are talking together casually and calmly. The next patrol is just on its way. So go! We sidle through between them. First slowly, then very fast. We're in luck. We're spotted and followed. But our head start is enough. Eventually, the pursuers give up the chase. The dim night swallows and hides us.

35.

Ice-cold days and nights follow.

The same hunger gnaws at us, and the same merciless cold plagues us. We get lost in this vast, almost uninhabited country. God grant that the direction is more or less right. We steer by the sun and stars. There are no excitements. No skirmishes, no acts of heroism, no encounters with Cossacks, just the one continuing struggle for our bit of life, for a warm place to sleep, food for us and for the horses. Just hope and courage to put off the end as long as possible.

On his own, neither of us could cope. We are fortunate to have each other. Fortunate that some baffling chance brought us together.

"You're like a brother to me," enthuses Konrad Klara.

"Well . . ." I laugh. "But not as wellborn as you."

"Drop the wellborn!"

We have one object in mind. To get home. Home isn't so far now. With every step, it's a little closer. Maybe another six hundred miles or so. But a few either way don't matter.

We've left Russia behind. In Polish territory, things are in slightly better condition. The big hunger and the perpetual cold seem to be past. There are farms dotted about here, with barns and stables. The nights are bearable dug into the straw or with the animals in the warmth of the stalls. The Poles are hospitable and help us where they can. Life becomes a little more humane.

The Russians haven't delayed. They didn't encounter any resistance, so they quickly rode on. After Napoleon. Past us, at some stage.

We're looking for the farm with the golden blond girl. The place where we spent the night and breakfasted on the march out here. I get shivers when I even think of it. The good food, and, well, the girl too.

We ride across a moor. This could be the place where I had my terrible bellyache. It's not such a dangerous place this time of year. Step off the path, and you don't risk your life. You don't sink into the marsh because it's all frozen. Now the forest ought to stop. The farm with the blond girl ought to be farther out in the plain. Of course, everything looks different in winter. And birch woods are birch woods. So it's not easy to find that one farmyard pressed into so much emptiness. Even so, we keep on looking. It could be here, it could be there, it could be anywhere.

The moor is finished. But the farm with the straw-blond girl isn't at the end of it. So it must have been a different moor. The birches and swamp holes and snowy places all look the same.

Evening is advancing. We worry we might have to spend the night in the open.

Wolves howl. Must be a whole pack of them. We should be wary of them. They're starved. In that condition, they will attack men and horses. We'd better ride around the wolves. But where exactly are they?

Ahead of us, there's something dark among the trees. The wolves? It's something bigger. Maybe a shelter for us, or something we can make a fire out of. Then we find nothing but a broken sleigh. No horses. Probably the driver was drunk and steered the thing into the trees.

We're curious and ride up to the sleigh. The wolves unwillingly withdraw.

We're aghast with horror. There's an almost naked man lying on the sleigh. Konrad Klara is the first to recognize him.

It's Krauter. He's curled up on the driver's bench, pale and dead, bent double, and frozen through and through.

He's lying dressed just in his shirt. Even the shoes have been taken off him. What's left of the wealth he stole? He's left with not even a pair of pants to cover his nakedness.

Strange. I'm not happy that Krauter's dead, but I do feel some relief. All of a sudden my hatred is gone. Krauter can't terrorize me anymore. Not with filthy puddles, thousands of balls of dung, and worn-out boots. He's lost all the power he had over me. Seeing him lying there, motionless in the sleigh, so far from any idea of life, I almost feel a little sorry for him.

We tip Krauter in the snow, and cover him over with the wreckage of the sleigh. Because of the wolves. It's all we can do for him.

Konrad Klara sighs. I wonder what he's thinking? Is he so affected by those frozen remains that were once alive? Or would he like to know what happened to his lovely Arabs?

We ride on silently into the breaking evening. I can't think of anything but the sergeant. I turn several times to look behind me. No, he really isn't following us anymore. It's just the wolves howling.

The horses change direction slightly and then put on speed. Can they smell a stable? That's right. Not much longer, and we see sparkling lights across the snow. There's a farm in front of us.

Thanks be to God.

We are kindly made welcome, can eat our fill, and even sleep in real beds. What more could we ask for? Nothing.

The farmer speaks excellent German. We learn from him that there aren't any Cossacks around at the moment, and that it's Christmas Day.

36.

With a small quantity of bread and meat, we ride off early the next morning. It's still bitterly cold. Apparently unusual for Poland, such an icy winter. Your breath freezes right away, and hiding my face in the fur doesn't help much. My eyes can't take the white glare. The best thing is to let my eyelids drop. An occasional blink to check that we're still going in the right direction. Everything else we can leave to the horses. They, too, have white beards. Their breath puffs out like clouds of smoke. The unusual frost over Poland seems to want to go on forever.

The farm with the girl with the blond braids must be somewhere else. We give up the search, and head due west. Toward home.

In the middle of January we reach Hohensalza. There we learn that the rest of the Wurttemburg army assembled here and set off home a week or two ago.

We are terribly tired and take three days to recover

from our exertions. One night, the Cossacks are suddenly there. This time we are properly taken prisoner. At least the Russians don't do anything to us, they don't even take away our horses. But we are detained in the town for another two weeks.

Konrad Klara says the Cossack units aren't interested in small fry like us. They're desperate to get Napoleon. They feel if they don't catch him, the war will never stop. Anyway, we don't present any sort of threat to them.

So we are finally allowed to go on.

There is a rumor going around that Friedrich the fat king of Wurttemburg has already distanced himself from Napoleon. What good to him is an ally who can't win his wars anymore? Napoleon has become a liability. Our king wants nothing to do with such a weakling. What he wants now is to hang on to the crown he got from Napoleon. To do that, he must enter into an alliance with someone powerful. Napoleon no longer qualifies. So, all of a sudden, he is against Napoleon. Initially, secretly. After all, one never knows.

The king of Wurttemburg has already been in talks with the czar of Russia. The czar's mother is his sister. That makes everything much easier. Konrad Klara puts me in the picture about all this stuff.

"What a fickle bunch!" I say. It's something our head farmhand used to say a lot. But it probably doesn't apply here, because Konrad Klara sends me an offended look.

37.

In the first days of February, we cross the frontier into Wurttemburg at Mergentheim. We are back in the kingdom, very nearly home.

I get such a ticklish feeling in my head and a tugging feeling in my chest. It's not like getting the butterflies before some great event, because I can't bring myself to feel happy at all. I am back again and must soon confront my farmer. That frightens me the most.

It's completely different with Konrad Klara. He's looking forward to being back at Lammersdorf, to seeing his mother and father and siblings — to being home, in a word.

I turn it around and around in my head: Where is my home? With the farmer, who doesn't want me? I no longer feel connected to my village or to the land.

A thread of melancholy dangles from my head down

into my belly. Really just on account of Konrad Klara. I know something is coming to an end. With the two of us. Soon each of us will go his own way. One without the other. He in his wellborn world, I in my simple world, in some stable or attic. Perhaps I should take Konrad Klara's head in my arms one more time, and tell him there is no one in the world whom I like as much as him. Words alone are not quite enough, he ought to be made to feel it as well. Clutch his hair, or something. But that would be a little more than crazy. The lieutenant count and me! In Russia it was like this, and now it's like that. I don't trust myself. My head is cooking.

The border guard takes us to the nearby barracks.

Our homeland doesn't offer us much in the way of a welcome.

A little first lieutenant demands Konrad Klara's saber. But of course he doesn't have one. Hasn't had one for some time. Then he's taken away, as if he's under arrest. And I'm led off in the opposite direction.

We're parted. Konrad Klara tries to say something to me, but the little first lieutenant pushes him away without a backward glance.

I could weep.

I'm in an empty stall, sitting next to a couple of ragged soldiers. They look at me curiously. Wearily, one of them asks me: "Russian campaigner?"

"Yup! You, too?"

He merely nods apathetically.

I feel so lonely without Konrad Klara.

Later, I'm thoroughly interrogated by a trim little staff captain. How and where I had been in Russia, under what colonels I had served, why I hadn't fought on to the end, why I had fled from the enemy, what I had been doing to get back so late? The last of the Russian campaigners had been back for weeks already.

I ask him where in Russia he had been.

He gets hopping mad at me and yells: "One more piece of your cheek, and I'll have you arrested!"

I suppress my anger and answer calmly: "The Cossacks took me prisoner just at the end."

"That you should not have permitted," he scolds me.

"What should I not have permitted? If I may ask the question, sir."

"To let yourself be taken prisoner!"

"I didn't let myself be taken prisoner. My lieutenant and I were taken prisoner."

"That comes to the same thing, and it's not good. His Majesty hates cowards, and he punishes everyone who was imprisoned."

"Oh, and why is that?"

"What do you mean by your question? I warned you not to be cheeky!"

After a period of silence, the staff captain adds: "His Majesty the king likes only victorious troops."

A boiling rage takes hold of me. Is that the reward for taking part in the most murderous war there has ever been? For a year of terrible hardship and privation? But I don't say so. I expect that would be an insult to the crown and high treason.

I could leap at the throat of that staff captain. And then at that of His Highest, Fattest Majesty.

I ask after Lieutenant Count Lammersdorf. That doesn't concern me and, anyway, he doesn't know, says the staff captain.

I am led back to the stalls. The other veterans see my fury.

"Calm yourself," a man urges me, with dirty rags wrapped around his feet, which he keeps scratching.

"Frostbite — itches like fury," he says, noticing my look.

From him I learn that of more than fifteen thousand Wurttemburg troops who set off to Russia with Napoleon's proud *Grande Armée*, only three hundred have come back alive. Most of them are done in, with frozen fingers and toes, and no use for anything anymore. There are even said to be cannibals among them, men who ate their dead comrades. Fifteen thousand have been hacked to pieces, clubbed to death, frozen, starved, or drowned.

"That's the price we pay for a crown for our Fat Majesty," remarks the man with the frozen feet. "But of course I never said that, and you didn't hear me," he adds quietly, looking about him cautiously.

I am taken to Ludwigsburg on a baggage cart. There I am inspected by a regimental surgeon. "Extraordinary," he remarks. "Most astonishing! Nothing wrong with the man, except undernourishment. Give him decent food for a few days, and he'll be able to serve."

I am immediately given a pale blue uniform. Corporal's uniform. How do they know I'm a corporal? I didn't tell anyone. Nor did anyone ask me. Someone must have made a record of the fact that I was promoted in Moscow. Was it my lieutenant? Probably. It's almost the only way it could have happened. How else would they know about it in Ludwigsburg?

If only I knew where Konrad Klara is, I'd feel so much better.

"The king needs soldiers again," is the word in the barracks. "Apparently, Napoleon wants another army from him." Even officers are talking like that, when they think no one's listening. "And where's the army going to come from?"

I am assigned to a new company of infantry. That's why I've been given such an impractical uniform. I could spend all day washing it, because that pale blue stuff always looks dirty. The boots are good. They hardly pinch at all, and once I've worn them in a bit, they'll be very comfortable. In any case, my toes aren't cold.

Shiny new six-pounder cannons are in the armory shed. I don't have to scrub them. Sergeant Krauter is no longer around, and a corporal isn't given scrubbing duties. And the dung balls in the barracks yard can stay where they are, too. Involuntarily, I sniff at my fingers, but they don't smell.

I wouldn't mind resting for a while, but I don't suppose I will get the chance.

Anything that can crawl and hold a rifle is spatch-cocked into the new regiment. It's all the manpower the king has. Everything was finished in Russia. All the horses and cannons, and the soldiers too.

So my meeting with my farmer is put off from week to week. I don't really mind, because at the thought of him, I get hot and cold shivers. What will the farmer say when he sees me? He can't have any idea that I'm among a mere three hundred survivors.

Sometimes I go crisscrossing the vast barracks yard, look here, take a peek in there, stroll around the officers' quarters. But I don't see any Konrad Klara. He would be in a different barracks. Too bad! I hope he hasn't fallen ill.

A little scrap of spring is shining from the heavens.

The air is fresh and light, young and clean and new. Everyone ought to feel happy that the winter is over, and everything is ready to begin again. What a beautiful world it is! No more cannon thunder, no broken bodies by the roadside, no puddles of filthy water, no glittering, murderous cold.

But my heart feels anything but light. So much of Russia is still attached to it. If only I knew why, and how I could shake it off.

And then I'm thinking about Konrad Klara a lot.

38.

It's snowing again, but it's barely worth mentioning. The cold doesn't hurt.

Life is bearable. I have decent clothing, hot soup, enough bread, the occasional piece of meat. At night I can sleep tolerably well, without being woken up all the time by dead bodies. I'm told I sometimes scream like a banshee in my sleep. But that's almost under control. I'm living in a well-regulated world now. Every day, Russia moves a little farther away. But I don't expect I shall ever be rid of it entirely.

New recruits arrive in the barracks. They seem to be getting scrawnier and more beardless all the time. I have to help train them. Because there are almost no more sergeants, and those six-pounders don't go off by themselves. It seems I shall be a sergeant very soon, in spite of my youth — and my staff captain doesn't know my true age, either. Curious. They say our fat king has learned a new tune. We returned Russian campaigners are not cowards after all. Because he needs every man jack whose fingers and toes haven't been frozen off in Russia.

Among my recruits is a puny fellow who comes from near my farmer. He's astonished that my name isn't Feuchter, but Bayh. And he's even more surprised to find me still among the living. Where the village scuttlebutt reported that I'd been taken out of the lists of the living by a cannonball at Borodino. That's what this young recruit tells me. My farmer hasn't been right in the head since his only son, Georg, suddenly died of quinsy, common or garden quinsy. That was too much for the farmer, and he isn't quite there anymore. That's what the recruit from my village says.

"How is he not quite there?" I ask the recruit.

"Well. He's just a little bit crazy. He's stopped working, he rambles over meadows and fields and woods, looking for his son, Georg, and his stable boy, Adam."

"Does he now?" That's all I want to say.

That's awful! At first I laugh unpleasantly. Then I become thoughtful and sad. I once respected the farmer like a father. But he disappointed me dreadfully. I can't forget that. Of course he deserves to be punished. Even without a royal judge, he's been sentenced. But I feel sorry for him, just the same.

39.

Barely two months later, I move off to war again, on my king's orders. We're going north, it appears, first to Wurzburg. There, our regiments are to rendezvous with Napoleon and his new army. No one quite knows whom the general is fighting this time. Perhaps against the Russians again, or perhaps against his erstwhile allies, the Prussians. One never knows, with Napoleon.

We move slowly northward. We don't seem to be in any particular hurry.

On the second evening, we're camping in a small village.

The staff captain and his two lieutenants are quartered in the castle. So that they can eat properly and sleep in a bed for the night. That's what is fitting for officers.

I want to take a look around the place. There are no enemies here. After all, we're still in our own kingdom. My six-pounder is securely sheltered, cleansed from the dust of the road, covered against rain or snow, and the sentries have been fixed. So I might as well have a little look-see.

The village has one street. Simple, old, little houses on it. I'm sure they all belong to the castle. I don't see a church, just a pub, the "Stag." There's a lot going on there. Maybe they have decent wine. Not the sort of swill that sours everything between your mouth and your waterworks. I'll try a quarter liter.

Half the artillery is squeezed into the small low-ceilinged room. A fug in the air that's really not breathable. The soldiers are coughing and sounding off about war and women. What else are they to talk about? There is only war. The wine's no good, either. A waste of the fine evening. I'd rather take a turn in the village or have a look at the castle.

The castle is easy to find. Just past the last of the houses, there's an alley of ancient lime trees and hidden at the end of it a big dark fortress with two turrets and lots of bay windows. A falcon sails out over the battlements. It all looks almost sinister. A dried-out moat and a mossy drawbridge. I wonder if it still pulls up? If the sun were shining, the old gray walls might be something like beautiful.

Three boys and a pretty half-grown-up girl come across the bridge. They wait to see who the new arrival is.

"Oh, it's not an officer, just a sergeant," says the girl

225

with disappointment. But I hear her just the same. After that the children speak French. It's rude of them. I don't understand what they're saying.

"No," I say to them. "I'm not one of your guests. I just wanted to take a little look at the castle courtyard. But it isn't necessary."

I am on the point of turning back, because the noble house intimidates me.

The children come nearer. They're talking to me again.

"You're welcome to come over the drawbridge," the girl tells me. "Don't be afraid. It's lasted three hundred years already. And you can have a look around the court-yard too. If you like."

My boots clatter over the planked bridge.

The girl and the older of the boys look familiar to me in some way. Nonsense, of course. Where would I have seen them before? I have never been here before. Even so.

The little boy is curious. He stares at me, takes me by the thumb, shakes it. "Have you got lice or bedbugs?" he asks boldly.

The girl pulls him away and gives him a scolding: "Don't be so naughty!" To me she says apologetically: "He doesn't mean it badly. He asks that of every soldier who ever comes here."

"That's all right." I set the girl at ease. "I don't have

any lice anymore. But a few months ago, I had a whole fur coat full of them."

"Just like my brother," the little fellow blurts out. "He had a fur full of lice. When he got back from Russia."

"Quiet!" the girl says to the boy.

Suddenly, I feel all hot and dizzy. I need to stop still. Is it possible? Of course it's possible. That's why the two children look familiar to me. The resemblance to Konrad Klara.

Hoarse with excitement, I ask: "Am I in Lammersdorf here?"

"Yes, of course," says the little fellow confidently. "Of course you are."

"And might your brother's name be Konrad Klara?"

This time the girl answers: "How do you know that?"

The children talk among themselves in great agitation. And in French.

The little boy takes my thumb again: "Then you must be the first people."

The girl pushes him away.

"Don't be so naughty," she scolds him, and she says apologetically to me, "He's referring to Adam and Eve."

"Our brother Konrad Klara has talked about you so much!" the children blurt out.

The older ones push me through a gate in the tower

into the yard, with the little ones toddling along on either side of us.

All together, they chorus: "Adam and Eve is here!"

A confused echo bounces back off the walls. Doors bang.

"Who's there?" A man's low voice. Then a woman's: "Who's there?"

Suddenly, the inquiring voice of Konrad Klara from a window nearer the top: "Adam Neve?"

"Hey, Konrad Klara!" I shout back, and I give myself a fright, because there's so much joy in my voice.

There's silence for a while. The three artillery officers peep out at the door, but then quickly disappear again. Probably they're just eating their dinner.

The children grab me by the arms again and drag me across the yard. The little one is clutching my thumb. They all want to ask me things, and chatter to me.

All at once, I'm not frightened of the noble house anymore.

Doors open and shut. People stream out into the courtyard.

A couple of torches are lit.

"Father and mother," says the girl. I am dragged over to a man and a woman. The man holds out his hand. Konrad Klara's father, surely. The woman looks at me long. Konrad's mother? I would think so. She comes very close to me, her eyes testing mine. It takes her a long time in the falling darkness. I think she would like to throw her arms around me.

But suddenly, Konrad Klara is standing in front of me. He is pale and gray-looking. Only his eyes look animated, flashing with joy.

"You should be in bed," his mother says anxiously.

"Mama," he protests.

"He is very ill," says the father. "Russia took everything out of him. But he's slowly getting better. It's taking its time."

Konrad Klara doesn't look well. I'm sad he's ill, and at the same time happy that I'm with him. I would like to show him that I like him. That he's more to me than a fellow soldier in a long and ugly war. But I don't know how to go about it. I could pat him on the back, or ruffle his hair, or embrace, or squeeze him to me very hard. How I wish I could do that. Well, of course I can't. The very thought makes the blood shoot into my head. It's not seemly, in front of his parents, his brothers and sisters, the servants.

Then I stop having to worry about such considerations.

Konrad Klara comes right up to me, grabs my hot ears, and pulls my head to his chest.

I feel so good, I forget the noble world all about me.

Then I come back to myself. Of course I don't want to show him how soft my soul is, and to keep him from noticing, I stammer back as dryly as I can: "Hey, Your Wellborn! Konrad Klara! Is that you? You don't seem to stink anymore."

There's deep silence. Did I say something wrong?

Then Konrad Klara laughs, and his parents laugh, and his brothers and sisters laugh, and all the servants and maids all around laugh.

"He's taking a laughing cure!" his mother says happily.

It's a wonderful evening, the most wonderful of my life.

The next day, as I move off to war with my six-pounder, I get the strange idea that I was really born yesterday, and that I'm probably not Adam Feuchter at all, but Konrad Klara's brother.

40.

Word gets around that the frail young sergeant with the six-pounders is a real Russian veteran.

They mean me.

I am gawked at, because I was in Moscow and because I have survived.

I am asked over and over again what this Russia place is really like.

"It's as big as the starry sky," I reply. "It stretches out farther than you can see, and it weighs heavy on your soul! But before you get to Russia, there's Poland, and in Poland there's the most beautiful girl in the world, with the loveliest straw-gold braids."

This book was art directed and designed
by Elizabeth B. Parisi.
The text was set in Centaur.
This book was printed and bound by
RR Donnelley
in Crawfordsville, Indiana.
The manufacturing was supervised
by Jaime Capifali.